To My Mother

Full-Page Illustrations

Lightning on Ice

JACK'S SKATES DUG IN, PUSHING HIM FORWARD.

IT WAS BEAUTIFUL BLACK ICE, SMOOTH and deep. The sharp steel skates cut into it with a powerful crunching rhythm. Standing behind the splintery pine boards of the hockey rink, Jack felt the sound in his flesh and bones. It was a wonderful sound, he thought, a sound that bespoke power and gracefulness and cold outdoor air.

The sound had different shadings and Jack could tell what they meant without looking at the hockey players. There was a short chop-chop of skates accelerating, that heralded the approach of a player gathering speed for a rush down the ice. There was a hollow, roaring sound that swelled in volume and then abruptly stopped, as a player checked his headlong speed with a sudden skidding movement; as his skates, which had been flying over the ice, turned sharply at right angles to their flight, slanting, digging in, sending up a shower of white ice chips.

There were slow, gliding sounds as players removed from the action of the game skated back to positions that

would be advantageous in the next scrimmage. There was the sharp, imperious blast of the referee's whistle stopping the play, slowing down the other sounds as the noon whistle slows down the factory. Then would come a face-off and the hickory sticks cracking savagely against each other would break the silence.

Then, without warning, there was an unpleasant sound, the sound of a body colliding heavily with pine boards. It was a collision of such violence that Jack seemed to feel that impact in his own body, the pain, the sick, nauseating feeling in head and stomach.

The whistle blew sharply. A small group of players gathered around a body that lay flat and motionless on the ice. Gripping the boards in front of him, Jack saw that the injured player was Johnny Nolan, the star of the Trent High School team, the fastest skater, the best player on the ice.

Now the winter air was filled with indignant voices: "Dirty hockey!" "Did you see that?" "He checked him right inta the boards!" "A board check—throw the rat off!"

Jack could see the referee motioning a player toward the side of the rink.

"That's the way, ref!" "Penalize the bum!"

But another voice yelled: "What's the matter? Can't the Trent sissies take it?"

"Oh, yeah?" called another voice. "Wanta make some-p'n of it?"

Watching the group of players, Jack saw with horror that there were bright red spots on the white snow chips. Nolan was bleeding. Now a man in a short canvas coat

and a fur collar was bending over the injured player. A boy with a white hat and a dark blue sweater with a big red T on it kneeled near him, squeezing a sponge into a bucket of water. Players stood around on their skates, some leaning on their hockey sticks, some skating in small circles, watching.

Suddenly there was a flurry on the ice and someone yelled, "Fight!" Two hockey players, one in the red, white, and blue jersey of Trent and the other in the yellow and brown of Cooper High, were arguing, pushing each other. Now one swung with his right, missed and closed in, clamping a headlock on the other player.

"Break it up!" yelled a spectator. "Sock him!" yelled another. "Throw 'em both off, ref!" yelled a third.

The referee's whistle was blowing frantically, and players from both teams were milling around, pushing, shoving, wrestling.

Jack watched closely, fascinated but with an uneasy feeling. A few minutes ago the hockey game on the smooth black ice had seemed a thing of grace and beauty. Now it was ugly, bloody—but equally interesting.

A man standing near Jack said, "It's a disgrace."

A feminine voice answered, "Good gracious! Can't they stop it? I've never seen anything so rough. Why, those boys have become savages!"

Jack turned and saw a woman in a fur coat, a woman he guessed to be about as old as his mother. Her face wore a shocked expression. Jack felt superior to her. You bet it's rough, he said to himself. I'm tough; I play hockey. He looked down at his skates. I wish they were hockey skates, he thought, tube skates like the fellows in the rink

are wearing. But that's a hockey stick I've got, he thought, consoling himself. It's a real hockey stick.

It had been a real hockey stick once upon a time. Now it was just a chewed and mangled mass of shreds and splinters held together with a nail and some adhesive tape at the critical joint where the stick curves into the hook that lies flat on the ice and holds and manipulates the hard rubber hockey puck. Jack leaned on this stick affectionately, as he had seen the players in the rink lean on their sticks, his two hands cupped on its end and his chin resting on his hands. He hoped the woman in the fur coat would notice. He glanced at her, but she was still watching the players.

"Oh, he's getting up," said the woman in the fur coat and there was relief in her voice.

Jack looked into the rink. The brawl had stopped; two fighters had been sent off the ice by the referee; the man in the short canvas coat and the boy in the blue sweater with the big T were lifting Nolan to his feet. Nolan's face was white. His black hair was wet and matted from the wet sponge. His nose, covered with white tape, was held high in the air.

"Only a bloody nose," said someone comfortingly.

"Maybe it's broken," said another.

"Oh, I dunno. Prob'ly just got the wind knocked outta him."

"Maybe. But those board checks are rough. They shouldn't be allowed."

"Aw, it don't hurt t'get tossed inta the boards once in a while; keeps the game from goin' sissy."

"Oh, the poor boy," said the woman in the fur coat.

Helped by the man in the canvas coat and the boy in the blue sweater, Nolan moved slowly off the ice, his legs limp, his skates dragging. The crowd applauded.

The whistle blew. The game went on. Jack counted the missing players. Two off the ice and in the penalty box for Cooper, one for Trent. He counted the remaining players. Gee, he thought, only seven players left; that is, seven skaters plus the two goalies. Gosh, what a lotta penalties!

Cooper had lost the squat defenseman who had thrown the fast-skating Nolan into the boards, in addition to a wing who had become involved in the fight. Trent had lost a wing because of the fight and now had a substitute in for its star center, Nolan.

"Come on, Trent, gang up on 'em," yelled a voice.

"Hold 'em now, hold 'em, Cooper."

"Get 'em while they're short a man, Trent."

"Hold 'em, Cooper!"

The symphony of sounds began again, the sharp, accelerating chop-chop of the skates as the wings got up speed for their flying trips down the ice; the rising, rushing noise that ended abruptly in a whining skid as racing skaters suddenly braked, the rhythmic scrape of the skates of players temporarily out of action.

Leaning against the boards, Jack could feel the vibrations of the game, the pulsing strokes of the sharp skates, the solid thumps as players bumped into the boards. Trent was trying hard now, but without its star, Nolan, it couldn't seem to co-ordinate its attack. Time after time the Trent forwards skated hard toward the Cooper goal and time after time they were turned back.

"Whad'ya think of that!" jeered a Cooper fan. "We got two men in the penalty box and still Trent can't score!"

"Trent would score if Nolan was on the ice," retorted a Trent fan.

"Oh, yeah?" said the Cooper fan.

"You had t'play dirty hockey to stop him," said the Trent supporter.

"Oh, we did, did we?" snarled the Cooper boy.

"Now take it easy, you two," said the man in the ear muffs who stood beside the woman in the fur coat.

"Dear me," said the woman in the fur coat, "these boys get so excited."

"Good for 'em," said Ear Muffs. "Gets it out of their systems."

"I should think they could get it out with a little less bloodshed," said Fur Coat. "I had no idea hockey made people so mad at each other."

Jack laughed to himself. That would be a good one to tell the neighborhood kids when he got home.

"It's a great game," said Ear Muffs. "Fastest game there is—great for the legs—great for the lungs."

"But a little hard on noses, I should say," said Fur Coat.

The referee's whistle blew, ending the second period. Cooper led 3-2.

Leaning on his stick, Jack hoped that the man in the ear muffs and the woman in the fur coat would see that he was a hockey player. Gee, he thought, it's the fastest game there is. Faster'n football or baseball or basketball. Why? Because the players were on skates, skating on ice,

and that made them go like the wind. Like I'm gonna go, thought Jack.

Looking at Ear Muffs and Fur Coat to see if they were watching, Jack pushed away from the boards of the hockey rink and started to skate. His left skate, pointed straight ahead, glided smoothly over the ice, while his right skate, acting as a propeller, kept up a continuous pushing action, digging into the ice, pushing him forward over the smooth frozen surface. Jack knew that this was not the way the players in the rink skated, but he also knew that when he had tried their way, pushing first with one skate and then the other, his balance failed him badly and he invariably fell flat on his stomach, spreadeagled on the ice. Now, with one skate as a pusher, he went fairly fast and straight over the ice, his ragged hockey stick held grimly in his hands, serving as a balancing rod. Going at full speed, Jack caught sight of a loose piece of ice just big enough to serve as a puck. With a great effort he swiped at it with his ragged stick. The loose piece of ice skidded forward over the pond, but the effort had cost Jack his precarious balance. His left skate shot out from under him and he felt himself falling. Mechanically he brought his stick over for support. It whacked against the ice, checked his fall for a second, then slid away, dropping him with a painful, jarring bump.

The black ice was now only two inches from Jack's face. He glared at it. There was no beauty in it now. It looked cold and hard and indifferent. Jack felt humiliated mentally and hurt physically. His hip hurt, his knee hurt.

He slid his cotton gloves over the smooth ice and pushed himself up.

Now he risked a glance in the direction of the rink and was pleased to find that the man in the ear muffs and the woman in the fur coat had their backs to him. Standing unsteadily on his skates, his second thought was that this meant they weren't interested in his skating, good or bad, and this thought did not please him. His hip ached, his knee ached, his ankles ached and sagged. His left skate tried to escape again. With a painful awkward wrench he brought it under control. Carefully he pushed forward and slowly leaned over to pick up his hockey stick.

Now he started back for the hockey rink where the referee's whistle heralded the start of the third and final period. Jack felt defeated and humiliated. He realized once more, as he had realized before after painful falls, how hard it was to learn to skate and how much harder it must be to go beyond that and be able to maneuver a hockey stick and a slippery puck. As he cautiously approached the rink, he saw out of a corner of his eye the figure of a boy teetering dangerously, straining to regain his balance, leaning too far over, falling in a heap on the ice. Coasting carefully to the reassuring support of the rink's pine boards, without turning his head for fear of upsetting his delicate balance, Jack felt immeasurably better—now his misery had company.

The referee was a stocky man with a black sweater and a red cap. One gloved hand held a whistle to his mouth, the other held the round black rubber puck, one inch thick, three inches in diameter. The two opposing centers

were facing each other, Nolan's substitute and the captain of Cooper High. They stood at right angles to their own goals, crouching, braced, their hockey sticks ready. The referee's hand left the whistle as he adjusted one of the centers' position. The center moved tensely, without looking up. Now the three figures were bunched together, the crouching bodies blending into a taut composition. Then the referee's left hand went to the whistle clenched between his teeth. He blew a sharp thrilling blast, two sticks whacked, the crowd yelled, the puck dropped, the game was on!

The Cooper center succeeded in sending the puck back to his own team. A Cooper defenseman stopped the skidding rubber and with a flip of his stick sent it slipping over to his right wing. The wing described a small circle, skates digging in, worked up sufficient speed, and started down toward the Trent goal. The Cooper center who had secured the puck for his team also swung down the ice, as did the Cooper left wing. Now the three Cooper forwards were moving down on the Trent goal in a well-organized offensive, their skates, scraping, flashing, flying.

Jack marveled at the skill and co-ordination of the players. At the same time he felt snug and secure behind the pine boards of the rink. The interior of the rink, he thought, was a terribly dangerous place where boys much bigger and brawnier than he skated at terrifying speed, crashed into each other viciously, sent each other sprawling, smashing into the boards, into the unbending steel of the goals, bruised each other, slugged each other, spilled red blood on the white ice chips. It was brutal, fascinat-

ing. A history teacher in school, Jack recalled, had talked about an arena in ancient Rome where gladiators were thrown to the roaring lions. This rink, thought Jack, was just as dangerous as the Roman arena. No one would catch him out in it, not for a million dollars.

The sounds beat upon his ears, the vibrations of the game went up through his hands clinging to the boards in front of him. Hockey was an electric game sending out impulses to the spectators lining the four sides of the rink. Jack's eyes were riveted to the flying Cooper forwards, the retreating Trent players. He watched Cooper's right wing skating fast toward the center of the ice. The Trent wing moved to cover the threat, skating backwards, his skates weaving in and out with an easy, graceful motion. Suddenly the Cooper wing carrying the puck skated sharply to his right, drawing the Trent forward with him. At the same time Cooper's center swerved slightly and now the crowd yelled, for the puck had flashed across the ice from the Cooper right wing to the Cooper center, and the latter, taking the rubber disc neatly on his stick, was through the Trent forward line and bearing down hard on the Trent defensemen. Quickly the Trent right defense moved between the onrushing Cooper center and the threatened Trent goal, where the goalie crouched with his thick goalie's stick and his heavy body pads and leg pads. The crowd yelled as the Cooper center, drawing near the Trent defense, passed the puck to the Cooper left wing who had followed along with the play. Now came a sharp, startled yell as the Cooper left wing, skating in fast, caught the puck on his stick, shifted it quickly to shooting position, and rifled it at the Trent

goalie. The hard puck left the ice, rising swiftly through the winter air and streaking for the Trent nets. But the Trent goalie had quickly sized up the play as the puck traveled from one Cooper forward to another, and had anticipated the shot. A second before the puck left the ice, the goalie turned toward the Cooper left wing, watched the puck streaking towards him, deftly caught it in the big leather gauntlet that protected his left hand, and dropped it immediately to the ice. Then, with a quick flip of his big stick, he sent it skidding out to a waiting Trent wing who gathered it in and started for the Cooper goal.

The crowd yelled: "Beautiful!" "Nice stop!" "What a save!"

Jack, marveling, agreed. What a stop that had been and what a game it was, this clash between Cooper and Trent with fast clever offensives, alert defensive play. Now, without a moment's hesitation, came the counter-attack.

The Trent forward taking the quick pass from the Trent goalie had a headstart on the Cooper forwards, who were caught going the wrong way. The Cooper forwards scrambled to regain their positions, but the Trent forward was too far ahead, ahead even of his own men, ahead and alone, skating hard toward the Cooper goal. Down he rushed on the two Cooper defensemen, one the stocky boy who had hurled Nolan into the boards. The Trent wing feinted to the left—the Cooper defense moved over. The Trent wing saw the open space between the two Cooper players and made for it. But the right defenseman caught himself and swung back fast to close the gap, just fast enough. The nutcracker closed. The two Cooper play-

ers caught the Trent forward between them and jammed him, jarred him, and dropped him on the ice like a sack of cement. The shock of the clashing bodies echoed over the rink. The Trent fans groaned for the victim. The Cooper fans cheered. The squat Cooper defenseman jumped over the prostrate body like an ugly frog, got the freed puck on his stick, and started toward the Trent goal. But the whistle stopped him. The Trent player had not risen but lay still on the ice, legs sprawled apart, arms flat and limp.

The crowd yelled, argued. The woman in the fur coat said. "This is awful—it's that terrible Cooper player again."

"Not this time," said Ear Muffs. "That wasn't dirty hockey. The Cooper player just bodychecked that Trent forward; it was perfectly legal."

"Perfectly legal," mimicked Fur Coat. "You make the boys sound like criminals."

"What I mean," said Ear Muffs, "is that it was a legitimate bodycheck."

"Ridiculous," said the woman.

"In other words," said the man, "the Cooper player will not be sent to the penalty box again."

"Penalty box!" exclaimed the woman. "Legitimate bodycheck! This game is for barbarians!"

"It's a great game," said Ear Muffs. "Develops the lungs, develops the legs, and toughens the spirit. See, look, no penalty."

The squat Cooper player was skating back to his position, and judging by the look on his face he was apparently very pleased with himself.

NOLAN SLASHED THROUGH THE COOPER FORWARD LINE. . . .

Ear Muffs spoke again: "That Trent player is all right. Look, he's getting up. See, he just had his wind knocked out." Ear Muffs' voice was reassuring. "See, he's all right; a little groggy, that's all. Don't get the idea that this game is brutal, 'cause it isn't. It's just fast, and when two bodies come together at high speed someone may get bumped around a little."

Fur Coat spoke firmly, her tone unchanged by the man's words. "I think it's a very rough and dangerous game," she said.

Listening, Jack wiggled his hockey stick, glanced over his shoulder, and gave the woman a pitying look. But, he thought to himself, she's right. I wouldn't go out on that rink for a million bucks, a trillion bucks. Gee, just that fall I took all by myself hurt like anything. I'll say this is a rough game.

The whistle blew. The game was resumed. Now Cooper attacked, its forwards hurrying the puck toward the Trent goal. The Trent forwards retreated, intercepted a pass, started toward the Cooper goal. A Trent wing skated fast, rushed toward the Cooper defensemen, then shot the puck low and fast at the Cooper goalie. The Cooper goalie stuck out his big thick stick; the puck cracked against it, was diverted to the side of the rink, thumped against the boards, bounced onto the stick of a waiting Cooper wing, and was once more started on its headlong journey.

There were cries of "Nice stop!" "What a goalie!"

"Notice that," said Ear Muffs to Fur Coat.

"Notice what?" said Fur Coat.

"Notice that the Trent forward took good care not to

let himself get too close to that Cooper defenseman. No
bodycheck that time."

"Thank goodness," said the woman.

"Afraid of getting hurt, I suspect," said the man, talking as if to himself.

Listening, Jack thought, I'd be afraid too.

Up and down the ice skidded the round black rubber
puck, slipping from one player's stick to another, sliding
flat and smooth on the ice, wobbling, rolling on its rim,
flying through the air. No one player seemed to be able to
control it, make it do his bidding, no one that is except
—the crowd yelled the name—Nolan!

The Trent star was skating out on the ice toward the
referee. The Trent supporters were yelling, calling, ex-
horting. "O.K., Nolan, let's go!" "That's the old fight!"

Jack caught the fever, felt like cheering. He heard the
man in the ear muffs say, "That's what I like to see, that's
guts."

"It's insanity," said Fur Coat. "Look at the poor boy,
how pale he is. Look at that adhesive tape all over his
nose."

"Just a scratch," said Ear Muffs. "Watch now."

They fastened their eyes on Nolan. And Nolan was
something to watch. The whistle blew, the puck dropped
on the ice, and Nolan was off. Somehow, like magic, the
puck was on his stick, glued to his stick. His stick patted
it and controlled it and made it obey. Deftly Nolan flicked
the puck, knocked it flat on the ice, not hard but with just
the right degree of strength. It obeyed; he was its master.
But, more than that, Jack could see Nolan was a skater,
a beautiful skater. When Nolan skated, the other players

looked like jerky and awkward puppets on strings. Nolan's force and energy were fluid. Effortlessly his body moved over the smooth black ice. His legs pumped power and speed into his body with a rhythmic one-two-one-two, his skates digging in, his slim tall body leaning forward. The speed increased from a clear, harsh chop-chop-chop-chop into a quieter, smoother noise—a powerful hum, the hum of a dynamo. But through it all flowed grace that an engine never had, the gracefulness of the human body, trained grace, developed, practiced, perfected. Here was the thrilling beauty of hockey, the eye-blurring speed of it, the art and grace of the skilled skater coupled with the courage and audacity of the hockey player.

Over the ice flew Nolan, down around his own goal to gather speed; to coil the spring, then to release it, fling it full in the faces of the other team. The two Trent forwards went with him, skating faster than they had ever skated before, trying their best to keep up with their flying center. And Nolan, sensing their efforts, weaved a little, cut slanting across center ice. He did not slacken his speed, but made a detour so that the straining Trent forwards, traveling a straight path, could almost draw abreast.

Then, like a hot knife through butter, Nolan slashed through the Cooper forward line, changing his pace, his direction, dazzling his awestruck opponents. Open-mouth they stared, stopped, and awkwardly pursued. Too late! With a burst of speed Nolan was through, and the Cooper defense was scrambling into position to stop this lightning attack.

Watching, Jack could see the expression on the face of the stocky Cooper defenseman. It was frozen in hard, determined lines. His skates scraped and stumbled, jumped and hopped like the flying hoofs of an ill-tempered colt. Anger and frustration were in their jerky movements. For Nolan was skating so fast that the Cooper defense was now by-passed and in hot red-faced pursuit, while the crowd's yells rose to a clamoring crescendo.

Jack, gripping the boards in front of him, saw Nolan swing wide around the Cooper defense. Too wide, he thought; now he won't be able to get in a shot at the Cooper cage.

Nolan had almost reached the end of the rink when he cut in sharply, and the squat Cooper defenseman in frantic pursuit lunged desperately with his stick and missed by a foot. Now the second Cooper defenseman rushed to the rescue, and as he charged down on Nolan Jack saw the strategy unfold. For Nolan, having drawn off the Cooper defense from the protection of their goal, now passed the puck neatly and swiftly to his own forwards who had skidded into position in front of the unguarded Cooper goal. With the Cooper goalie watching Nolan, it was child's play for the Trent right wing to take the skidding puck on his stick and whip it deep into the Cooper nets. The crowd let out a wild roar. The score was tied 2-2. Nolan had done it.

"Now *there*," said the man in the ear muffs, his voice vibrating, "there is a hockey player. Did you see that. Did you see him draw off the Cooper defense and set it up for his own wings? Gosh!" Ear Muffs smote the boards

with his leather gloves. "That's hockey, that's big league stuff!"

"I will say," said the woman in the fur coat, "that the boy is a wonderful skater."

He certainly is, thought Jack. Boy, that was terrific! The play was still dancing before Jack's mind: Nolan's rush down the ice, his maneuver to outwit the Cooper defensemen, his quick pass out to his wing, then the goal. He looked out over the boards at Nolan who, oblivious to the noise from the crowd, crouched near the referee, his body tense, his face, color in it now, impatient and yet cool and confident.

The crowd was hushed. Nolan had startled them, stirred them, warmed them to a pleasant, exciting expectancy. The whistle blew again. Once more Nolan beat the Cooper player to the punch, batting the puck over to his own wing, getting it back on a pass, skating toward his own goal to pick up speed. He skated in that easy, graceful way of his, leaning against the ice, his hockey stick held in one hand with the puck resting securely against it. He came forward now, up by his own defensemen, darting over into center ice swiftly and smoothly, weaving through the Cooper forwards with a sudden burst of speed. As he swooped down on the Cooper defense, he feinted to the left, getting the squat Cooper player off on the wrong foot. Then, completely reversing his direction, Nolan audaciously darted between the separated defensemen into the hole his maneuver had created. Back into the breach jumped the stocky Cooper defenseman. Too late. Nolan was through like a flash, in

all alone on the Cooper goalie, drawing that padded individual out of his cage by faking a shot. And Nolan flipped the puck almost contemptuously into the empty nets, leaving one Cooper man openmouthed, another angrily whacking the ice with his stick, and the Cooper goalie flat on his padded stomach where his desperate dive for the puck had deposited him in a humiliated heap.

The Trent fans were pounding each other on the back, cheering, yelling. The mouths of the Cooper fans were open but no sound was coming forth.

Ear Muffs was crying: "Beautiful! Beautiful! All by himself. A solo!"

A solo, thought Jack. That's what it was, all right. A solo. Perfect.

"And did he split the Cooper defense!" crowed Ear Muffs. "Right in half."

He certainly did, thought Jack, right in half. Went right between 'em.

"And did you see how he pulled the goalie out of his cage?" exulted Ear Muffs. "Then flipped the puck in like a griddle cake into a frying pan. That Nolan is really a hockey player."

"He's a very good skater," said the woman in the fur coat. "Very good indeed."

Boy, if I could only skate like that, thought Jack.

The whistle blew, the game went on. But Jack had a feeling that it was over. He was right. Nolan's solo had been the climax. Now Nolan was on the sidelines as the coaches changed their forward lines. And without Nolan the game seemed to lose its spark. Players stumbled and

fell, lost the puck too quickly, passed it inaccurately. They were exhausted and they showed it. Their energy had been drained from them by their frantic dashes up and down the ice, in attack, in pursuit.

There were a few more scrimmages, a few more shots that thudded against the goalies' thick pads; then the whistle blew and the game was over. Trent 3, Cooper 2.

The crowd cheered; the perspiring players cheered each other; people started skating and walking over the ice to the clubhouse for hot coffee and chocolate. The man with the ear muffs and the woman in the fur coat left with the crowd, skating smoothly and sedately over the ice.

Jack pushed after them, one skate coasting, one shoving. Off to the right, he saw a group of players heading toward the clubhouse. Hurrying, pushing hard, he was able to cut across their path. In the middle of the group was Nolan. Watching the Trent star, Jack's eyes were wide and full of admiration. He saw close-cropped brown hair, blue eyes, a firm jaw, a mouth that curled up a little when it smiled. The adhesive tape on Nolan's nose gave him a reckless, gallant look. His red-white-and-blue uniform completed the heroic picture: the blue jersey with red and white stripes on the arms; the short white hockey pants with a blue stripe down the side; the long thick blue stockings with red and white stripes; the wonderful skates of thick tough leather and shiny strong aluminum and steel; the padded leather gauntlets that Nolan carried carelessly in his right hand. Nolan was wearing a tan polo coat. A dark blue sweater with a red T was knotted around his neck. He was skating effortlessly, yet others in the group seemed to be scurrying to keep up with him.

Jack saw someone skate up fast, dash into the group, clap
Nolan on the shoulder, and cry, "Nice going, Johnny
boy!" Nolan smiled, the group closed around him again,
and the Trent star and his followers moved on.

Left behind in their rapid pace, Jack came to a stop.
His ankles were aching so much from his exertion that he
had to drop to his knees on the ice. As he knelt, his eyes
following the laughing group surrounding the hero, his
attitude might have been mistaken for a gesture of hero
worship or a prayer that a novice might some day become an expert. And perhaps it was either of these two
things or both; but mostly it was because of a painful
ache in weak ankles.

HE POND WHERE THE TRENT-COOPER game had been played was big enough to be called a lake. And for that same reason, because of its width and its depth, long steady spells of cold weather were necessary to freeze it thick enough for skating.

Just a few days after the game, warmer weather arrived and the deep black ice began to melt. But Jack and the boys he knew were determined to play hockey. They ignored the signs that read DANGER NO SKATING, found a cove shielded by small sloping hills, sat down on the bank, and exchanged shoes for skates.

For goals in this pick-up game they used bundles of discarded clothing—coats and sweaters. They guessed at the right width of the goals and at the distance between them. The oldest of the players, a boy named Poletti who was a high school freshman, supervised these activities.

Poletti had a real rubber puck, a hockey stick neither split nor ragged, and a pair of shiny red shinguards. Of all Poletti's equipment Jack thought that the shinguards

were the most wonderful. They were made of fiber board that seemed as hard as a rock, and when a hockey stick whacked against them, the sound was loud and impressive. Their shiny hard surface was curved to shape over the shinbone. Inside the cavity were two stout elastic straps that separated the sensitive shin from its protector, forming an air cushion which would absorb the hardest whack of a hockey stick. These shinguards were fastened around the leg with two leather straps, one at the top, one at the bottom. Then they fitted close and secure, and the thick felt cup that guarded the knee fell snugly in its place. Watching Poletti strap on his shinguards, Jack thought, If I had a pair of those, oh, boy! As for Poletti's brown leather shoes and his skates—tubes of light aluminum riveted to the shoes, blades of strong sharp steel riveted to the aluminum tubes—Jack could only stare and sigh in admiration.

Hopefully Jack joined the group on the soft ice of the cove and watched Poletti and another boy choose up sides. First one boy was picked, then another. The boys chosen skated happily away, cutting circles, skidding to a stop, showing off their skill to each other, proud that they had been chosen so quickly. Jack waited, fearful. No one pointed to him. Four boys had now been chosen for each team and the group had broken up. Timidly Jack pushed after Poletti. "Hey! Kin I play?"

Poletti looked down from above his shiny shinguards. "We already got five on each team."

"Yeah, but . . ."

"Wait until somebody drops out," Poletti interrupted. "Someone'll quit; someone'll maybe get hurt." He started

to skate away and then stopped short. "Say, wanna be goalie? Wanna play goalie for us, huh?"

Jack said nothing. He did not want to play goalie for Poletti's team and yet he wanted to be one of the players.

"Hey, Schulz!" Poletti yelled at the other captain. "O.K. with you if this kid plays goalie for us?"

Schulz looked and saw a small slight boy with wobbling ankles. "O.K." he shouted. "But we can lift then."

"Whad'ya mean, ya kin lift?" cried Poletti. "Ya heard what we said before. No lifting. This kid ain't got no pads."

"Well, why doncha give him yours?" gibed Schulz, grinning.

"Oh, yeah?" said Poletti. "And have youse guys whacking me across the shins? Fat chance." Then, changing his tone, he added, "O.K. Let's go. Hey! Shoot that puck over t'me."

Jack stood in the goal between the two bundles of clothing. He was sorry now that he had spoken to Poletti. He knew how hard the rubber puck was and how fast some players could shoot it. He knew that as long as it stayed flat on the ice there was nothing to fear, but if it were lifted on a stick with a quick snap of the wrist, lifted and sent flying through the air, it would have the speed and destructive power of a rock aimed and thrown by a big league pitcher.

This was a pick-up game. There was no cohesion in it and little teamwork. It was dominated by the two big boys, Poletti and Schulz. When they didn't have the puck on either of their sticks, they were yelling at the other boys to pass it to them. Only when they were breathless after a rush down the ice did the other boys have a

chance at the puck. It was a ragged, uneven game, a game of shinny.

Schulz got the puck and skated toward Jack's goal. With ease he outmaneuvered the forwards, but Poletti charged up to meet him. Schulz tried to skate past Poletti, failed, and sent the puck skidding toward Jack. Jack saw it coming but his awkwardness gave him no time to move. The puck struck his right skate and knocked it out from under him. He teetered on one skate and then colapsed. A loud laugh went up from the other players. Poletti swooped in, turned sideways, and skidded to an ostentatious stop that sent a shower of ice chips over his prostrate goalie.

"Nice stop, kid." Poletti was grinning. "Hey, gimme the puck. Where is it?" Poletti's hockey stick poked at Jack's ribs.

"Hey, take it easy," said Jack. He was ashamed of his collapse and yet a little proud that he had somehow stopped Schulz's shot. He fished under his body for the puck, found it, and pushed it toward Poletti. Poletti stabbed at it and skated noisily away.

Jack got to his feet and brushed off the ice shavings. He stood up uncertainly on his skates, slipped, caught himself, steadied himself with his mangled stick, and managed to stand straight again, guardian of the goal. He heard a small cheer from the other end of the ice. Poletti had scored.

"Hurray," said Jack weakly. He felt that he should say something.

Poletti was skating back now, grinning proudly; even his skates seemed to swagger with pride. Poletti's hand-

picked team was patting him on the back, saying, "Nice work, nice going." Poletti's face was flushed and serious, full of confidence. He turned his skates sideways and skidded to a showy stop. "That's only the first one," he said loudly; and then to the other team: "Come on, youse guys! Whad'ya doin' with that puck, eatin' it?"

"It's lost," said a voice. And Jack saw players poking their sticks in the mud and snow on the shore.

"Aw, for pete's sake!" cried Poletti, skating toward the searching party. The loss of the puck detracted from his triumph. "You guys lose that puck and I'll bop somebody!"

"Whad'ya shoot it so hard for then?" said Schulz. "You're the one who lost it."

"Oh, yeah?" said Poletti.

"Yeah," said Schulz. "The goal was wide open. We haven't got a goalie like you guys, y'know."

"O.K., O.K.," said Poletti, stepping gingerly off the ice on the toes of his skates. "Gee, this stuff'll wreck a guy's skates."

"Walk on the toes of ya skates then," said Schulz.

"That's what I'm doin', dope," said Poletti. "Listen, I know how t'take care of my skates. I was walkin' on the toes of my skates before you even got yours."

"I got it," yelled a voice.

"Swell," said Poletti. "Throw it out; come on, throw it out."

"Oh, no," said the finder of the puck. "It's our puck; we're bringin' it up. Go on, Poletti, give us a chance t'bring it up."

"O.K.," said Poletti, "but we haven't got all night. Sup-

pose a cop comes. We ain't supposed to be skatin' here, ya know."

Standing in the goal, Jack heard Schulz yell "Over! Over!" and watched the boy who had found the puck obediently pass it to his captain. Schulz had the puck now and was pushing it ahead of him as he came toward Jack's goal, skating with jerky awkward movements. His skates chewed the soft ice at a rate far out of proportion to the forward movement of his body, like a car's wheel spinning in an icy rut. Suddenly there was a piercing, ripping noise. Schulz's right skate sank into the soft ice and down he went with a thump. Poletti whooped with glee, darted in on the cursing figure, and stole the puck away. He swept down the ice, brushing aside his smaller opponents, and scored another goal.

Laughing with the others, Jack watched Schulz get to his feet. Schulz was still cursing and vainly trying to brush off ice water that had soaked into his sweater and pants. To the boy nearest him Schulz snarled: "What's so funny? Anybody could trip on this lousy ice. Come on, gimme the puck."

"Two to nothin'!" yelled Poletti triumphantly. "Whad-'ya doin', Schulz, playin' hockey or swimming?"

"Shut up," said Schulz, and then, turning to a teammate, "Pass that puck."

Jack saw the look on Schulz's face. It was a warning.

Schulz took the puck again and started down with his hasty, wasteful motion, chopping into the soft ice with his skates. Again Poletti faced him and again Schulz veered off. Suddenly Poletti gave a sharp cry. But it was too late. The hard puck, lifted by a vicious snap of

Schulz's stick, whistled through the air and struck Jack squarely on the shinbone of his left leg. He felt a pain such as he had never felt before, a pain that sent its throbbing waves through the nerves of his body, up through his stomach and chest, down through his arms. He let out an agonized yell and sat down moaning, gripping his shin. Players gathered around him, some silent, some offering sympathy. Poletti glared at Schulz. "I told ya no lifting. What's the big idea?"

"I didn't mean it," said Schulz, but it was plainly a lie.

"Whad'ya mean ya didn't mean it? Anyone can tell when he's gonna lift."

"Well, why don't ya give the kid your shinpads?" said Schulz.

"He wouldn't need 'em if ya'd stick to the rules," said Poletti.

"Oh, nuts to the rules," said Schulz.

"O.K.," said Poletti, "we'll see about that. I'll lift one right inta your big trap."

"Oh, yeah?" said Shulz.

"Yeah," said Poletti.

"Hey, kid!" Poletti spoke to Jack. "Lemme see it."

Jack had been afraid to pull up his trouser leg and look, for fear that the shinbone would be sticking out of the skin, but he obeyed Poletti. Even the light touch of the trouser leg, as it dragged over the injury, hurt. But Jack was relieved to see that though there was a red and blue bump as big as a small egg, there was no sign of the shinbone.

"Gee," said Poletti, "look at that bump."

Everybody was staring. In a way Jack was glad that the

SUDDENLY POLETTI GAVE A SHARP CRY.

bump was there; it justified his anguished reaction to the accident.

"Here, kid," Poletti picked up a hunk of ice. "Put this on it.".

The cold ice stung. Part of the bump turned white under the icy pressure.

Some of the other boys began to skate away and scramble for the puck; their scramble led them out of the cove.

"Hey, look out for that puck," Poletti called. "That's thin ice out there. I don't care if you dopes fall in, but that puck cost dough." He straightened up. "Hey, kid, tell ya what I'll do." Poletti leaned over and fumbled at the leather straps on his shinguards. "I'll let ya wear these. O.K.?"

"Gee," said Jack. "Oh, boy!"

"Here," said Poletti, "got a handkerchief? Wrap it over that bump. That's right. Now strap 'em on this way, see? O.K.?"

"You bet," said Jack. "Boy, these are swell."

"Yeah," said Poletti, getting up and turning away. "Hey, come here with that puck. Come on, let's get going. Score's 2-0."

"Whad'ya mean, 2-0!" cried Schulz. "I just got a goal!"

"Didn't count," said Poletti. "You lifted. We said no lifting. Remember? O.K., bring it up."

The pattern was repeated. Schulz brought the puck up, skating in his hurried, awkward way, trying to dribble, shifting the puck awkwardly from one side of his stick to the other. This time Poletti crouched, knees bent, hockey stick held across his middle, and let Schulz draw

near. Then he took two steps, thrust his knee and his hip into Schulz's body, and knocked him sprawling. Schulz's stick clattered to the ice, skidded for several yards, and came to a stop. The puck followed it. Poletti flipped Schulz's stick out of the way with a contemptuous flick of his own stick and gathered in the puck. As Schulz screamed imprecations, Poletti took the puck through Schulz's teammates and scored for the third time.

Jack watched Poletti skate back up the ice. Schulz, on his hands and knees, grabbed his stick with his right hand and swung it viciously like a scythe at Poletti's legs. Poletti's skates swerved sharply and the swinging swipe of the stick missed by inches.

"Naughty, naughty," jeered Poletti in a falsetto voice.

Schulz cursed again.

Poletti's mood changed. "Aw, shut up!" he yelled. "What'sa matter? Can't ya take a bodycheck? Naw, ya can't. But the kid took one of your dirty shots right on his shin. Go on, get up and play hockey."

Eventually Schulz did get up and play hockey. Snarling, he snatched the puck from one of his teammates and again started his noisy, awkward rush toward the goal Jack defended.

Jack watched tensely and as tensely Poletti crouched. They both knew Schulz was boiling mad and they expected the worst. Angrily Schulz tried to feint Poletti out of position. When his attempt failed, he skated to the right and got as near as he could to the goal without coming into contact with Poletti. Then, drawing his stick back with the puck nestled against it, he flashed it forward and snapped the puck on its way. The warning cry from Pol-

etti reached Jack a split second before a jolt on his shin. The puck hit the shinguard and dropped to the ice, rolled a little, fell flat and stopped. Astonished, Jack quickly recovered and gave the puck a push toward the onrushing Poletti.

"Nice stop, kid! Nice save!" cried Poletti, taking the puck on his stick. Grinning, Poletti described a semicircle, skillfully crossing one skate in front of the other, holding his stick in his right hand and pushing the puck ahead of it.

"Hey, Schulz," he called as he finished his turn and straightened out for his run down the ice, "did ya see the stop the kid made? Did ya, Schulz?"

Schulz held back his answer. He waited until Poletti drew near, chased him for a few strides, and then whacked him sharply across the shins. Poletti let out a yell that echoed in the ice-covered cove. Instinctively he stopped and viciously swung his stick. Schulz ducked and the stick whistled over his head. Poletti swung again, lower this time. Schulz turned quickly and took the blow against his rump. "Ouch," he said, adding quickly, "O.K. We're even."

"Yeah?" said Poletti, dropping on one knee and rubbing his shin.

"Aw, come on," pleaded Schulz. "I was just trying to pokecheck the puck away from you."

"You were not," said Poletti, rolling up his trouser leg. "Your stick wasn't even aimed at the puck; it wasn't anywheres near it. Look at that bump. Boy!" There was a little pride in Poletti's voice. The bruise, like Jack's, was big and discolored.

"It's pretty," said Schulz, grinning.

"Pretty!" yelled Poletti. "I'll . . ."

He grabbed his stick and swung at his tormentor. Schulz was wise enough to stay out of range and the stick described an arc, found no target, and clattered harmlessly to the ice. "Just wait a minute, just you wait," said Poletti.

"What's eating you?" said Schulz. "We're even. You socked me and I socked you."

Meanwhile one of Schulz's teammates had picked up the puck. Skating forward, the boy tried to dribble it, moving his stick from one side of the puck to the other. He lurched, tapped the puck too hard, and sent it skidding toward one of the players on Poletti's team. Now Schulz entered the fray, seizing the puck with a characteristic maneuver, a stumbling rush toward his opponent, a blunt whack with his stick. Then, with the puck on his stick, Schulz hopped and jumped, stumbled and scrambled toward Jack and his shiny shinguards. But Poletti had anticipated Schulz's action. Dropping his trouser leg over his swelling bruise, he had skated into a position across Schulz's path. Now he crouched with his stick knee high, closely following Schulz's clumsy dribble, and at just the right moment lashed out with his stick. Poletti's stick found its target, the puck skidded free, and Poletti yelled, "Now there's what you'd call a pokecheck!"

Schulz, chagrined, watched the puck skim over the ice. Then his chagrin vanished as he saw the rubber disc slide serenely out of the cove onto the thin ice of the pond. Watching the puck and realizing what this would mean to its owner, Schulz broke into a laugh. "O.K., wise guy!"

he cried. "There's your pokecheck and there's your puck.
You go get it—and have a good swim!"

And with this parting remark Schulz turned on his
skates and retreated toward his own goal, where he plop-
ped down on one of the piles of clothing, a big grin on
his face.

Poletti was silent. He stared at the puck lying on the
thin black ice of the pond.

"I'll get it," said one of Poletti's teammates, a small
boy with a freckled face.

"No." Poletti shook his head. "If you fell in and got
drowned, I'd get the blame."

"Lemme go," said Jack half-heartedly.

"Not with my shinguards on," said Poletti.

"I'll take 'em off," said Jack.

"I was only kiddin'," said Poletti. "I'll go. I gotta go.
That's the only puck I got."

Gingerly Poletti pushed forward, testing the ice that
lay between him and the puck. A dull booming crack
rose up from the pond like the sound of a distant explo-
sion.

"Gee," said one boy, "did ya hear that?"

"Look, you kin see it," said Jack.

The players looked. A crack an inch deep appeared in
the ice of the cove.

"Boy! We'd better get moving," said one player.

"You ain't kiddin'," said another. "This ice is melting
too fast to suit me."

"Don't get scared so easy," said Poletti. "This ice is
plenty thick."

"It's not thick enough for me," said one boy, picking

up his sweater from the pile and skating toward the shore. Maybe I'd better get off, too, Jack thought. He reached toward the pile of coats and sweaters, then stopped and looked. A boy yelled. Poletti was skating out over the thin ice toward the puck.

Poletti advanced on the puck in a series of swoops. The ice sagged and creaked ominously. Poletti stopped swooping and skated fast and straight for the puck. He reached out with his stick, swung around, and sent the rubber disc skimming over the thin ice to the safety of the cove. A boy cheered. Jack stared. Poletti was returning. The ice was sagging dangerously, rising up and down beneath him like a rippling snake. Poletti was skating uphill and downhill over the creaking ice. A boy yelled, "Come on, Poletti. You kin make it."

Jack could see the expression on Poletti's face. It was tight with determination and excitement. He'll make it, thought Jack fearfully. Poletti came on fast; then suddenly tripped, let out an anguished cry, and fell, crashing through the thin ice into the deep, icy water of the pond.

The boys stood paralyzed. Then they broke into excited cries and skated in excited circles. "He's up," someone shouted. Poletti had pulled himself onto a ledge of solid ice and was pushing himself up with his arms. Suddenly the ledge gave way and Poletti dropped back into the icy water. Cakes of ice ground around him, seemed to promise support, and then sank under his weight.

Schulz skated to the rim of the thicker cove ice. Jack thought, Maybe he'll rescue Poletti. But Schulz came to a stop and yelled, "Take your skates off, Poletti! They're weighin' ya down!"

POLETTI FELL, CRASHING INTO THE ICY WATER OF THE POND.

Poletti was defiant. "These skates cost ten bucks!" he cried.

"All right then, drown, you dope," said Schulz, skating away.

Jack did not stop to analyze whether it was Schulz's remark or Schulz's shot that had hit his shin that caused his decision. As the other boys watched in astonishment, Jack made for Poletti. Pushing awkwardly with his right skate, coasting with his left, he moved determinedly out over the cove ice. When he reached the thin ice of the pond, he dropped to one knee and, getting flat on his stomach, wriggled forward with extended hockey stick. He ignored the warnings of the other players.

"Grab my ankle," he cried to them, and someone followed, lay down, and grabbed Jack's ankle. Then another joined the human chain and another, and now there were four boys anchored to Schulz, who was kneeling on the thick safe ice of the cove.

Jack slid farther out nearer Poletti. Poletti thrashed against the heavy icy cakes, pushed them aside, and fought his way to the solid ice. Jack stretched, Poletti strained. Then Poletti managed to grasp the end of the hockey stick which Jack extended toward him.

"O.K. Pull" cried Jack. "Everybody hold on with two hands!"

Slowly, painfully, Poletti came up out of the icy water onto ice that held under his weight, over the ice of the pond to the thicker ice of the cove, where he lay at last soaked, dripping, safe.

"Thanks!" he gasped. "Thanks a lot!"

Schulz was grinning. "That was pretty good, wasn't it?

A human chain. Say, we could get our pictures in the papers."

"And get pinched for skating here? Listen, Schulz, I heard what you said when I was out there and when this kid here—" Poletti pointed to Jack "—and the other guys were lying on thin ice. You were sitting nice and safe back here where it's thick."

"I helped pull you out," said Schulz indignantly.

"From a good safe distance," said Poletti, "and when I get my wind back, I'm gonna knock your teeth down your throat just on general principles."

"Oh, yeah?" said Schulz.

"Yeah," said Poletti. "Yeah, yeah, yeah!"

But by the time Poletti got his wind back, got up on his skates and began to wring out his dripping clothes, Schulz had wisely departed.

Jack was sitting on a log unlacing his skates. Poletti and two other boys built a small fire, and steam rose from Poletti's wet clothes as he stood in colored shorts and held his pants near the crackling flames.

"Hey, kid," said Poletti to Jack, "which way ya going?"

"By the clubhouse towards Harley Street."

"Well, wait a minute and I'll go with ya," said Poletti.

"O.K.," said Jack. He was pleased and flattered. After all, Poletti was a high school freshman and moreover he had tube hockey skates, shinguards and, by virtue of a rather risky and damaging bit of salvage work, a hockey puck.

Jack slid the hook of his hockey stick through his skates, hoisted them over his shoulder, and started to-

ward home by Poletti's side. He was happy and proud.
A day that had started miserably, with an assignment of
goal tending and a painful bang on the shin, had turned
out extremely well; by express invitation he was walking
home with a big boy, a high school boy, a good hockey
player.

"What's your name, kid?" said Poletti.

"Jack."

"Jack what?"

"Jack Taylor."

"Where d'ya go to school?"

"Longfellow Grammar."

"What grade?"

"Sixth."

"Where ya goin' to high?"

"Trent, I guess. Is that where you go?"

"No. I go to Commerce High."

"D'ya know Nolan?"

"I've heard of him."

"Boy! Is he a hockey player!"

"Yeah. And does he think a lot of himself! Trent fellas
say you practically gotta get permission to talk to him."

"Gee," said Jack. He pondered this for a minute, then
asked, "Is Nolan going to college?"

"Oh, sure," said Poletti. "The great Nolan has to go to
college. But first of all he's goin' to prep school—some expensive joint up in Maine called St. Barnes Academy."

"St. Barnes?"

"Yeah, they got swell hockey teams up there. And why
shouldn't they? They got ice, nice and solid all winter,
not like it is here." Poletti looked down at his soaked

trousers, black with ice water, his shoes in which his feet made squishing noises. "I wish I could go to St. Barnes," he said sadly.

"So do I," said Jack. "Solid ice all winter—gee! That would be swell. Not like the old pond here."

"Yeah," said Poletti. "Tomorrow there won't be any ice at all. Of all the lousy weather—just when it was thick and smooth."

"Yeah," said Jack.

"Come on," said Poletti, "let's go to the clubhouse and get somep'n to eat and a hot chocolate. Boy, could I use a cup of hot chocolate!"

Jack said nothing.

"What'sa matter, Jack?" said Poletti. "You in a hurry to get home?"

"No," said Jack. "I haven't any money."

"But this is on me," said Poletti. "I got half a buck. We'll have hot dogs with plenty of mustard, and chocolate and plenty of marshmallow. O.K. with you?"

"I'll say," said Jack. And to himself, he added, What a day this has turned out to be!

IT WAS POLETTI WHO TOOK JACK TO A
small shallow pond shaded by tall cedars and pines from
the melting rays of the sun. And here under Poletti's
sometimes patient teaching, Jack began to learn how to
play ice hockey. But first of all he learned how to skate,
pushing with both feet instead of just one, taking smooth
instead of jerky strides, one on the left skate, one on the
right, gaining good control of his balance so that he could
glide on one skate without wobbling. Gradually he
learned the right technique: first, left skate forward and
a little to the left, right skate pushing; then, right skate
forward and a little to the right, with his left skate pushing, his weight shifting from one skate to the other. At
first his ankles bent in so far that his skates became worn
and discolored where the leather scraped along the ice.
At times he felt as if he were skating on his ankles. But
gradually the muscles in his ankles, aching, complaining,
sagging at first, grew tougher and stronger. Jack's skates

began to take a stronger bite into the ice as they sent his body forward faster.

Between and during pick-up games on the shaded pond, Poletti taught Jack how to cut—to turn by putting one skate in front of the other, changing direction without losing speed. Jack liked to cut; it was a very satisfying feeling to get up speed by this maneuver and to go so fast that players trying to capture the puck were quickly outdistanced. Jack learned how to skate backwards, holding his stick above his knees and parallel to the ice, using it as a balancing rod, weaving his skates in and out. All of this seemed very hard at first and at times irksome. Sometimes Jack thought it would be easier to skate by holding one skate still and pushing with the other instead of getting power and propulsion from both. Sometimes he thought he would never learn how to skate properly. But there were other times when he felt himself skating fast without fear or worry about falling and getting hurt. Once in a while now Poletti and the other older boys who dominated these pick-up games would pass the puck to Jack and let him take it down the ice on his own, a great privilege. And although this usually happened when the older boys were either exhausted or hemmed in by opponents, it was an indication of progress and Jack was pleased and proud.

He looked forward eagerly to the games on the pond, to that exciting time when he would sit down, lace up his skates, and then take those wonderful first few strides out on the ice, feeling the ice glide by underneath, feeling the wind against his face. In school he would keep

one eye on the big black hands of the classroom clock
and one eye on the weather outside the window. Out the
window a black cloud might gather in the northwest and
move slowly up into the clear blue sky. Jack would fidget
in his seat and exchange notes with another hockey
player: "Think it'll rain?" "Is there skating on the big
pond?" "I had my skates sharpened the other day." "Wait
till you see my new hockey stick."

Slowly, very slowly, the hour hand would move toward
three. At long last the bell would ring, loud and piercing,
the bell that signaled the end of school. As the word "Dis-
missed" came from the teacher, Jack would leap from his
desk so quickly that he often banged himself in the pro-
cess, and charge for his cap and coat. In twos and threes
the boys would set out for the big pond, hockey skates
dangling, hockey sticks bouncing up and down on their
shoulders. Down the street by the neat lawns and drive-
ways, the wood and brick houses with their storm doors
and windows, across the macadam parkway, and there
before them, at the foot of a sloping embankment, was
the big pond, its frozen surface dotted with skaters.

The sight of it stretched out before him never failed to
send shivers of anticipation through Jack as he stood at
the top of the embankment, looking at the white snow
and the evergreen trees, the smooth ice and the gliding
skaters. Then he would hurry down the slope, impatient
to feel the ice under his skates and the puck on the hook
of his hockey stick.

If the ice on the big pond were too thin and the danger
signs were up, the boys scattered in search of other places

where they could play hockey, concealing their destinations for fear of overcrowding a secluded pond big enough for just one hockey game.

There was an almost endless variety in the ice. Sometimes it was soft and white and the sharp points of the skates sank into it, tripped the hockey player, and sent him skidding along the wet ice on his stomach. The ice might ambush him with a long deep crack, a crack that would catch a player's skate and bring him down with a bruising, jarring bump. Once in a while there was white snow ice, made by snow melting on the ice and freezing quickly, and on the snow ice the black puck stood out sharper than ever.

There were all kinds of ice and all kinds of ponds on which it was to be found, some ugly, some pretty like the little pond Poletti had introduced to Jack. Here it was one afternoon, two months after the game in which he had played goalie, that he came with his skates and stick, found no older boys bullying or dominating, and to his surprise and delight found himself scoring more goals than any of the other boys. He had learned to skate, and his legs now carried him forward in a rhythmic, well-balanced motion that sent him fast and sure over the ice. He could stop suddenly by turning his skates sideways on the ice, sending up a satisfactory shower of ice chips. He could cut, putting one skate in front of the other in a time-saving turn. He could skate backwards, weaving his skates in and out as a sculler weaves an oar in the water. And he was so engrossed in the game and pleased with his new ability that he did not see Poletti appear on the shore. The older boy stood and watched for a moment as

Jack, carrying the puck, dashed through the players on the other team. Then Poletti, sliding his skates off his hockey stick, yelled, "That's O.K., Jack. You're gonna be a hockey player."

Jack Taylor was eleven years old at the time.

THE FIRST YEAR JACK WENT OUT FOR hockey at Trent High School was a very bad year for a newcomer. He was too light to play defense, and the three positions in the forward line—left wing, center, and right wing—were firmly occupied by juniors and seniors in both the first and second string lines that Trent's coach used.

When the call for hockey players came, Jack hopefully took his new tube skates and stick to school. But it was obvious to him from almost the first blast of Coach Boney Ward's whistle at practice that it was going to be next to impossible to play for Trent that year.

At practice the coach played his two regular defense-men in front of the veteran Trent goalie. Then he formed three lines of forwards, gave them the puck, and sent them down the ice to try to take the puck past the de-fense, past the goalie, and into the cage. The first two lines formed by Boney Ward were boys he had coached the previous year. These veteran lines worked smoothly.

The third line was made up of Jack and two other new boys. They were nervous, stiff, and awkward. Each time they brought the puck up the ice they lost it. Sometimes, ignominiously, they lost it long before either of the defensemen so much as made a face at them. The puck would roll off their sticks, slide far out of reach, sometimes hide itself under the boards of the rink, to leave one of them scratching for it shamefacedly with his stick, like a clumsy puppy scratching for a bone wedged under a fence. When the three novices did succeed in getting the puck as far as the veteran defense, the defensemen simply dabbed at it with their sticks and shook it loose. Their attitude was aloof and contemptuous. Jack thought it would have been less humiliating to be bodychecked and smacked down against the hard ice. Then, thought Jack, his line might be pitied and not just ignored.

When the coach cut his squad and posted his list of players for the coming season, Jack's heart beat fast, his hands grew warm and moist. He looked long and hard at the list of names, the names of boys who would get full uniforms, and at the end of the year dark blue sweaters with a big T on them. His hopes rose up as he studied the list thumbtacked on the school bulletin board, and then fell with a jar that felt like a physical blow. His name was not on it. The blow had such an effect that he lost all his former feeling for his new skates and his new hockey stick. They seemed like symbols of defeat.

When Trent played its first game, Jack's skates were high and dry in the hall closet at home. It snowed and he got out his sled and went coasting down a snowy hill after school. Once he tried skiing. In both sports he felt

exhilarated in the downhill rush and unexcited the re-
mainder of the time. When he wondered why he was disappointed in skiing and coasting, he reasoned that they
were not games, that you couldn't plan an attack or a
retreat or a counterattack in them; you couldn't score
goals and, above all perhaps, you couldn't have the thrill
of winning something, beating somebody. The ice melted,
the snow melted, and Jack was depressed.

Then a cold spell blew in from the northwest. The red
mercury in the thermometer at the kitchen window
dropped to 30, 25, 20 degrees and stayed there. A thin pane
of clear glass appeared on the big pond. It thickened and
became strong enough to hold skaters. Out of the hall
closet came skates and hockey stick. On the shore of the
pond, Jack laced up his skates with the old anticipation
and excitement. He had not made the Trent team but he
could skate pretty well. When sides were chosen now for
pick-up games among boys his own age, he found himself among the first players to be chosen. It redeemed
some of the lost hope. And by the end of the winter when
the ice melted for good, Jack was skating well enough
and fast enough and gracefully enough so that older
skaters, men who had once been hockey players and who
retained a love for the sport, would stop and watch the
pick-up game and nod their heads and say, "That boy can
skate."

That's what Coach Boney Ward thought the next season
at Trent, when his first forward line had graduated and he
was left with the task of building up some new players.
Boney stood at the side of the rink, claw-like hands pos-
sessively clutching the pine boards. He had motioned

Jack into center position on one of the forward lines he was trying out, meanwhile shaking his head sadly over his depleted material. Boney had done his selecting in a cold tone that reflected his discontentment over the new crop of candidates. He had rolled off the names disinterestedly. "Schwartz, Newman, Taylor; all right, you fellas, form a forward line. Taylor, you take center." Boney had put Jack at center by chance and not because he thought Jack would be any better at the key position than Schwartz or Newman.

"Whad'ya shoot, Schwartz?" said Boney.

Schwartz hesitated and Boney muttered to himself: "He don't even know what I'm talking about. What a fine bunch of rookies this is! What a swell team I'm gonna have this year!" Then aloud he said: "Well, Schwartz, which is it? Do you shoot left or right? Or, in other words, do you raise the puck off the face of your stick from the right side or the left side when and if you are in position to shoot the puck?"

Schwartz, more confused than ever, said, "Both, sir."

Jack and Newman laughed. Boney made a face. "Never mind the laughs," he said. "This isn't funny by any means. Not when I think of the team I'm gonna have this year. Come now, Schwartz, make up your mind." Boney had an inspiration. "When you play baseball, whad'ya bat, left- or right-handed?"

"Leftie," said the red-faced Schwartz.

"O.K. Fine! Then take left wing." Boney whacked the boards. "That puts you on the right side, Newman. You do shoot right, don't you?"

"Yes," said Newman. "Yes, sir."

"Good," said Boney. "Fine! Great! I'm getting a break. O.K., here's the puck." Boney pulled a new puck out of his coat pocket and tossed it on the ice. It landed flat with a smack. Jack nervously tapped it with his stick, thinking, Oh, boy, a brand-new puck!

"When I give you the signal, you go," rasped Boney.

The new line grouped together, passing the puck to each other. A minute went by and then Boney yelled, "All right, we're gonna start. Let's have three lines goin' down the ice. Make your attack, double back, and go down again. And when you lose the puck down there, when the play is over, don't fool around. Just skate back up the ice with your line and start down again. O.K. Let's go."

Turning to the manager of the team, Boney said: "This is gonna be good. We've got two lettermen left on the forward line and one on defense, and these new guys don't know whether they shoot right or left. We're in for a tough season."

The manager, a youth named Maloney, put a serious look on his face and nodded. Secretly the manager didn't care very much one way or the other, having no worries or responsibilities about making the team, getting his teeth knocked out by a skate, or explaining why he had lost the puck just as he reached the opposing goal. And having shown his skin-deep concern, Maloney pushed his little white hat with the red T back on his head and settled down to enjoy the practice session. It was a lot of fun, he thought, watching the boys struggling to get a place on the team. It meant so much to them. They tried so hard. They were so happy when they made the team

and so crestfallen if they failed to make it. Manager Maloney looked out into the hockey rink from his safe and comfortable position behind the boards and thought, I'm glad I'm not out there.

Just then his reverie was broken by Coach Ward. "Who's that kid playing center on the second line?"

The manager, instantly alert, looked at the boy playing center in the line just coming up the ice, failed to recognize him and, to gain time, said, "Which line, Coach?"

"Which line d'ya think?" said Boney sarcastically.

"You mean the kid sorta slight, medium height, with the black hair parted on the side?" said Maloney.

"Yes," said Boney.

"Now let me see," said the manager, pulling a folded piece of paper out of his overcoat pocket. "I've got all the names down here and the positions they were trying for."

Coach Ward, silenced by this display of efficiency, shifted his feet which, despite overshoes, were getting chilly from close contact with the ice.

"Let's see," said the manager. "Schwartz, he's the kid who didn't know right from left. Newman, he tried out last year and didn't make it. Er, Taylor, that's who it is, Taylor. He's a junior, Coach. Came out for the team last year and was dropped when you cut the squad." The manager spoke the last sentence with just the slightest of rising inflections, the gentlest of implications.

Boney Ward caught the hardly noticeable reproof and decided it was not worthy of attention. Instead he said in an aloof tone: "Didn't make it last year, eh? Taylor's his

name? Oh-h-h, yes, I remember. Taylor, eh? Hmmm. The boy's a good skater, a natural skater; easy style, fast, graceful. Handles himself well. A little light though, but maybe he's wiry. We'll see when he takes a bodycheck or two. And look at that!" Boney's tone rose. "Look at that, Maloney."

The manager looked and saw Jack push a weak shot at the goalie.

"Oh, no; oh, no," said Coach Ward. "That will never do. Never. No use getting down there if you can't shoot. But"—Boney whacked the boards with his hands—"the kid's a good skater, a natural."

At practice Jack still felt unsure of himself, self-conscious, tightened up. His skates didn't seem to act the way they should, the way they acted on the big pond in the pick-up games. Once they got in the hockey rink where Trent practiced, the same skates that flashed freely over wide open spaces seemed to become stiff and awkward.

I can skate better than this, Jack would tell himself over and over again. Was it the hockey rink he was unused to? Was it the tension of waiting for that list to go up on the bulletin board? Jack couldn't figure it out. But he knew he was doing better than the previous year.

The two defense players were taking his line seriously now. The new line was coming down the ice fast, and they were getting the puck to stay on their sticks until they got within shooting distance.

It's better, thought Jack, but is it good enough?

The doubt remained until one day Newman came up to Jack at the lunch hour in school, slapped him on the

back, and whooped, "The list's up—we're on it! We're in!"

Jack's hand, holding a half pint of milk, shook a little as he aimed the straw in the bottle toward his mouth. A mouthful of lettuce and peanut butter sandwich stuck in his throat. He coughed, his face reddened.

"Are you sure?" he asked eagerly.

Newman looked indignant. "Of course I'm sure," he cried. "You, Schwartz, and me, we're gonna be the second string line. Come on, let's find Schwartz and tell him."

Now the tension was off. Now the fun began. Equipment was issued: red-white-and-blue jerseys; short white pants with blue stripes down the sides and thick felt pads inside that fitted over the hip bones; long, blue woolen stockings with an elastic band at the bottom that fitted over the instep. There were shinguards as hard as stone, and wonderful leather hockey gauntlets with stiff padding for each finger.

Jack marveled at the equipment, worn as some of it was. He marveled at the bundle of hockey sticks, smooth, unblemished, that the assistant manager carried under the manager's patronizing direction. He marveled at the stack of new pucks that Maloney stacked and counted in a nonchalant way. It was an organization, thought Jack, a real hockey team with a coach and equipment and a regular hockey rink to practice in. It was the Trent High School hockey team and Jack Taylor was on it.

The first opponent on the Trent hockey schedule was Hurlbutt High. The game was to be played at the Plaxon rink, an artificial pond made by hosing tons of water into a slight depression excavated in warm weather with a

steam shovel. The shallow water at Plaxon's froze quickly and good shade kept it frozen. So there was often skating at Plaxon's when there was no skating on the big pond. It cost money to skate there, and only a few afternoons of the week were reserved for hockey. These days were seized upon well in advance by such enterprising young men as Manager Maloney of the Trent hockey team.

At 2:30 p.m. one Friday afternoon, the Trent team assembled in the locker room downstairs in the high school building. There was a great deal of noise and confusion. It was typical pre-game tension. Jack felt it throbbing through him. It was exciting, nerve-racking, pleasant.

"Where we gonna dress?" Newman asked the question.

"Over at Plaxon's." Dick Whittemore, senior and captain of the Trent team, answered. And Whittemore's tone was friendly, without the slightest hint of condescension. "Come on, you guys," he said. "Let's get going. We wanna get in some practice before the whistle blows. You been practicing how to shoot, Taylor?"

"Yeah," said Jack.

"How's it going?"

"Oh, a little better."

"Swell! Once you get the hang of it, you'll be surprised how simple it will seem." Whittemore caught sight of the manager and said: "Hey, Maloney, where ya going with all those sticks? Got a good one for me?"

"Sure, Dick." The manager's voice was as smooth as maple syrup. "Which one d'ya want, Dick?"

Captain Whittemore reached into the bundle and pulled out a long smooth stick with a red paper label that said "Wrightson's Pro Hockey Stick." Grasping it

with his right hand, he flipped it up and sighted along its length. "It's not warped," he said. Then he placed the heel of the stick on the cement floor of the locker room and rested the stick on its hook, the part that propels the hockey puck. Moving it slowly a little to the right, a little to the left, Whittemore saw that the stick was shaped so that it slanted a little to the right as it rose from its base. "It's right-handed," he said, sounding very sure of himself, "and it's just about the right length. I like 'em nice and long. Tape that up for me, will you?"

"Sure thing, Dick," said the manager.

Whittemore handed the stick back to the manager with a lordly gesture and turned to his second string line. "O.K., fellows, let's get going. You fellows are riding over to Plaxon's in Maloney's car."

This is something, Jack thought. It matters to someone as important as Whittemore that I practice my shooting and that I get to Plaxon's rink on time. Something very big and important is happening and I am a part of it.

This feeling lasted through the ride to Plaxon's while the second string line kidded and sang in the back seat of Maloney's car. It lasted through the dressing room excitement at Plaxon's, where grammar school kids and high school boys looked with awe and interest at the Trent team, its manager, its coach, and its equipment. The exhilarating feeling lasted through the hurly-burly in the dressing room, where Jack pulled on his blue jersey and laced up his skates.

"Get those lacings tight, fellas," ordered Boney Ward, "A loose skate is as bad as a sprained ankle."

Jack's sweaty hands worked over his long, leather laces,

pulling the eyes of the shoe so tight that his ankle felt as if it were in a brace. He stood up on his skates and his ankles felt firm and strong. The only weakness he could feel was in the region of his stomach.

With the other Trent players, Jack clumped out over the wooden boards placed on the cement floor to keep skates sharp. In his right hand he held his hockey stick loosely and with nonchalance, in imitation of Captain Dick Whittemore. Jack wondered if Whittemore, clumping authoritatively at the head of the procession, felt any tension; the Trent captain looked the picture of self-assurance as he sauntered toward the rink, chatting with Coach Ward and occasionally acknowledging a cheer from an admirer.

"Let's go, Trent," called a voice from the audience.

Jack felt pleased when he heard the voice. It was addressed to the Trent team filing out to the rink, to Whittemore, to Schwartz, to Jack Taylor. He felt pleased and proud and very nervous.

He felt better when he got on the ice of Plaxon's rink on his tight sharp skates and practiced with his line, passing the puck back and forth with Newman and Schwartz, taking practice shots at Kelly, the Trent goalie. He felt worse when pre-game practice ended and they skated over to the bench where Boney Ward was waiting. Boney said: "I'm starting the second line—you, Taylor, you, Newman, and you, Schwartz. Go out there and show me what you can do."

Jack felt numb. He didn't believe his ears. He glanced incredulously at Newman and Schwartz, and they returned the glance with equal incredulity. A good-sized

crowd had gathered around Plaxon's rink, and they were creating a rising volume of sound, a racket of whoops, cheers, and threats. Frantically Jack thought, I'll make up an excuse, say I have a pain in my side. No, I can't. Look at Newman and Schwartz. They're ready to go. I've got to go. If I could only sit on the bench for a while and let Whittemore start. I'd be all right later if I . . .

"Come on, Taylor," ordered Boney Ward. "Get your line out there."

Boney Ward's hand was on Jack's shoulder. It was a heavy, hard hand. It felt cruel, thought Jack, like a claw. The fingers of the claw bit into Jack's shoulder. "Just play it safe, Taylor. Once you lose the puck, check back. Cover your defense. O.K. Get out there now. Good luck!"

The referee was beckoning. Jack skated toward him through a mist that seemed to rise off the ice. The yelling of the crowd grated on Jack's ears. The referee's face was a blur and so was the face of the Hurlbutt center. Jack heard the referee say, "Around this way, Trent," and felt the referee's hand on his shoulder. He thought, I can't even face off right. What'll the coach think? I wish my stomach would settle down. I wish my ankles would get steady. I wish . . .

He crouched over. The whistle blew sharp and penetrating. The grinding sound of it went in his ears, through his brain, and down through his body. He saw a black shadow flash before his eyes. The puck. Mechanically he whacked at it. Too late. The Hurlbutt center had beaten him to the draw.

Dimly in the distance he saw the Hurlbutt forward line circle, cut, get up speed, come forward. Drumming in his

ears was a crashing of confused sound—the sharp, surgical
sound of the skates of the Hurlbutt forwards rushing toward him, the rising clamor of the crowd. The tension
rose with the cutting sound of the onrushing skates. Gripping his stick tensely, following the sliding puck, Jack
saw the black disc passed by Hurlbutt's right wing to
Hurlbutt's center.

The center is going to try to bring it through, thought
Jack. He's my man; I've got to get that puck away from
him.

The Hurlbutt center came rushing forward, skating
fast, dribbling the puck. Jack skated backwards, his stick
held crosswise just above his padded knees. He weaved
a little, then lashed out with his stick. Crack! The stick
hit the bull's eye, knocked the puck free from the Hurlbutt center, and sent it rolling behind him as his rush
carried him past Jack. Jack's skates dug in, pushed, hurled
him forward. Just a few feet ahead of him lay the puck,
free, flat, and beautiful. He heard a cry from the Trent
crowd. "That's the way, Taylor! Jump 'em, jump 'em!"

He had jumped them, jumped the Hurlbutt forward
line which, carried down the ice by its rushing impetus,
was now completely out of the play.

Jack's skates bit into the ice. He gave the puck a quick
push, skidded it ahead of him on the ice, caught it on
his stick, patted it from one side of the hook to the other.
He was skating fast now, but his skates were still a little
unsure. He was still tense and the skates seemed to slip
on the glassy ice. Jack felt that he should be skating twice
as fast. Out of the corner of his eye he saw Newman and
Schwartz on the flanks, skating down with him. Jack

HURLBUTT'S TWO DEFENSEMEN CLOSED IN ON JACK.

skated straight for the Hulbutt defense, then cut a little to his right. Hurlbutt's two defensemen, faced with the choice of covering Jack's maneuver or guarding Newman on the wing, closed in on Jack. Jack seized the opportunity and sent the puck over to Newman, his left wing, hard, flat, right on Newman's stick. Jack saw Newman take the pass nicely and then felt a jarring thud, a painful bump. He was on the ice and sliding head first toward the end of the rink, sliding so fast and so helplessly that he felt as if he were in a greased chute. Instinctively he put out his hand. There was a loud crash and he hit the boards at the end of the rink. A sharp pain shot through his shoulder.

Somewhere from far off came the dull yell of the crowd. Jack got to his knees, got on his skates, looked back at the cage. No score. The Hurlbutt goalie must have blocked Newman's shot. Jack's head began to clear. Only seconds had passed but they seemed like minutes.

The Hurlbutt goalie had stopped the shot and cleared the puck out to his wings. They had taken it and were now charging down on the Trent defense. Schwartz and Newman had checked back. Jack thought, I should be with them. He picked up his stick, lying near by on the ice, and skated back toward his own goal. He heard a voice from the crowd yell, "Get those splinters out of your brain, Trent." He resisted a desire to turn his head and answer.

As he skated by the Hurlbutt defensemen he thought, Which one of those guys hit me? He didn't wonder long. Hurlbutt's right defense, a big boy built like a barrel, grinned maliciously at Jack and sneered, "Come again."

Jack skated swiftly ahead, silent. His shoulder ached. He knew Coach Ward would see how far out of the play he had been knocked. Newman's shot had been blocked, but Jack felt that if he had stayed on his skates he might have been able to whack in Newman's rebound. Some of the tension had been broken by the action Jack had been through, but in its place had come a feeling of sour dissatisfaction.

Suddenly Jack saw the puck lying loose on the ice a few feet ahead of him. Without thinking, he hooked it onto his stick. Instantly he heard the sharp, shaming blast of the referee's whistle. He was offside. And his impulsive capture of the puck had prevented a breakaway attack by Newman who had knocked it free. Newman said as much but without anger in his voice.

Jack thought, Why doesn't Newman say what he really thinks, instead of being so polite about it?

By stopping the play, the referee had allowed the Hurlbutt forwards to get back into position. Now there was a face-off, the whistle blew, and Newman sent the puck to Jack.

"Let's go, Taylor!" cried Mason, Trent's left defenseman, as Jack skated near him with the puck. Jack dug his skates into the ice, felt his speed pick up, and said to himself, I'll circle behind our own goal; no, that's a waste of time. This is far enough. I'll cut across in front of our own goal.

He skated in front of the Trent goal, dribbling the puck, and to his horror lost it with an awkward movement of his stick and sent it skidding toward the Trent goal.

Kelly, the Trent goalie, saw the puck sliding towards his cage. With a quick movement of his big stick he stopped the puck in the nick of time and quickly registered his annoyance by shouting, "Hey, Taylor! For gosh sake!" At almost the same time a sarcastic voice in the crowd yelled, "Attaboy, Trent! Score against yourself if ya can't score against Hurlbutt!"

His face red, his whole body sick with embarrassment because of his mistakes, Jack watched Kelly flip the puck over the ice to Newman who had come skating in. Newman said, "Come on, Jack," and Jack gripped his stick hard and dug into the ice.

The color was drained out of his face now and his lips had become a thin straight line. He felt the speed flowing from his pumping heart down into his legs and into his skates. He sailed by his own defense, caught up with Newman at center ice, slackened speed a little to stay parallel with his own wing, and took a pass from Newman. Then he turned on the speed and flashed by the Hurlbutt center, leaving him crouched futilely, his stick across his knees.

Bearing down on the Hurlbutt defense, Jack flipped the puck over to Schwartz and watched the Hurlbutt defense split open, one man to the right, one to the left. He saw the puck flash back from Schwartz's stick, took it neatly, seized the opening ahead of him, and with another burst of speed skated through the middle. Through the slim opening of unobstructed ice between the Hurlbutt defensemen he sped in on the Hurlbutt goalie, faked a shot, watched the goalie dive to stop it, dribbled around him, and backhanded the puck into the empty cage—goal!

The crowd exploded in a roar. On the Trent bench Boney Ward exclaimed with surprise and delight, "That's what I like to see! Take it on the chin and come back. O.K., Whittemore, get your line out there and sew this game up while they're still groggy."

Jack was tingling. The tension, the sick despair, and the sudden glory had been like hot and cold showers that left him glowing. Newman and Schwartz skated over and patted him on the back as the teams got ready for the face-off. Goalie Kelly, indignant and angry just a few minutes ago, whacked his big stick on the ice in hearty approbation. Mason, the defenseman, called, "Nice going in there, Taylor." To complete the triumph, Captain Whittemore, skating out onto the ice with the first string line, calmly drawing on his gauntlets for the contest ahead, came over to Jack and said, "That's the way to play hockey, Jack." It wasn't Taylor any more. It was Jack and from Whittemore, too. That was the best compliment of all.

The assistant manager threw a sweater on Jack's shoulders and added a topcoat. Jack's breath turned into steam in the cold air, but under the sweater and coat he was warm. He had never felt better. Coach Ward spoke and Jack listened closely. "I don't have to tell you, Taylor, what you did wrong. You know those two mistakes you made as well as I do; in fact, making them the way you did you'll probably never forget them."

Jack nodded.

"Always circle your own cage when you wind up," said Boney. "Whenever the puck is near your own cage, see to it that it stays behind the cage or at an angle that

makes a shot impossible. As for the puck you picked up when you were offside, the referee underlined that mistake with his whistle. Try to keep the ref's whistle quiet, unless you get a signal from me when I want to send new men in." Coach Ward was talking out of the corner of his mouth, his eyes still focused on the game.

"There it is!" he cried suddenly. "Take it."

The Hurlbutt goalie was on his knees. The black puck skimmed over the ice from Whittemore's stick, flashing in front of Hurlbutt's goal, sliding swift and straight to the Trent left wing. The rubber disc caromed off the wing's stick, flew through the air and landed in the nets behind the Hurlbutt goalie, falling to the ice in the cage. Trent had scored again.

Coach Ward, gripping the boards of the rink, relaxed. His voice, which had been hoarse and excited as the scoring play developed, became normal again. He went on talking to Jack.

"You could have avoided that bodycheck, the one that knocked you out of the play and cost you a chance at a rebound. Get that puck to behave automatically, so you won't have to watch it all the time. You set up your first play all right; but when the rebound from Newman's shot bounced off the goalie's pads, just waiting for someone to whack it in, you were flat on your back against the boards and Schwartz was doing a waltz with the other defenseman. But don't worry, you'll learn. When you scored, you scored good. And what was better was the way you came back after that bad beginning. If you can do that, you've got what it takes. If you're gonna play hockey, you'll need what it takes."

T HE GAME WAS OVER. TRENT HAD WON,
five goals to two. Jack's line had scored again in the second period. The dressing room at Plaxon's rink was warm
and noisy and very cheerful. Sweating, grinning figures
slapped each other on the back. The steamy air rang with
triumphant cries. The Trent players were boisterous and
happy. They had approached their first game as all hockey
teams approach it, with wonder and doubt. If they lost,
their season's record was ruined at the beginning. If they
tied, it was neither one thing nor the other. But if they
won, they were off to a good start. And they had won.

Somebody brought in hot cocoa and crackers.

"Hey, look at this! Bet we wouldn'a got this if we'd
lost."

"Mmmm, thank you."

"Not for me, I'm too thirsty. Gimme an orangeade or
anything—coke, root beer. I musta lost ten pounds out
there."

"Aw, cut it out."

"Whad'ya mean, cut it out? You guys who play defense just sit back there all afternoon. Us forwards are scrambling all the time."

"Oh, is that so?"

Coach Ward came in and the noisy dressing room became quieter. Boney hitched up a trouser leg and put one foot on a wooden bench. "Fellas, that was pretty good. You came through O.K. Frankly I had my doubts about this team—we didn't have many lettermen left, and it isn't easy to build a team without veterans. And I don't know yet whether we have one or not. We've only played one game. But"—Coach Ward dropped one foot to the wet cement floor and replaced it on the bench with the other foot—"you did pretty well out there today. You fellas in the second line—Schwartz, Newman, Taylor—showed up well. You kept attacking. That's what I like to see. Keep that puck down there in the other team's end of the rink. Get that puck away from their forward line and hold on to it." Coach Ward paused. "Kelly, you played a nice game in goal except for that second one that got by you."

Kelly grinned sheepishly.

"Nichols," the coach continued, "you and Mason were O.K. on defense. Those bodychecks you handed out were good. Whittemore, I don't have to speak about your line because you know what you have to do out there and you do it; you learned that last year. But what I want to say to all of you is this." Coach Ward planted both feet on the floor, put his hands in his coat pockets, and hunched his shoulders. "Last year we had a good team but we dropped two games. Unfortunately, those two games

were the most important games on our schedule—Cooper and City High. They were both close, but close isn't good enough. This year let's get out there and win those games. Before we played and beat Hurlbutt today, I didn't think we had much of a chance. But what you showed out there today may be good enough. Get those two games for me, fellas, and I'll give you the Metropolitan Championship." Coach Ward took his hands out of his pockets. "O.K. That's all. No practice tomorrow. Rest up."

AN I GIVE YOU A LIFT, JACK?" IT WAS
Mason, the new defense player. He was a boy of medium
height and solid build, with thick brown hair and a big
grin that showed straight white teeth.

"Sure, thanks. You going near Harley Street?"

"I can," said Mason.

They walked toward the parking lot. "Here it is," said
Mason, grinning and pointing his hockey stick at a faded
coupe. "It has an engine 'n everything."

"As long as it runs," said Jack.

"Oh, it runs—sometimes. 'Course I have to spend a lot
of time fixing it up but it usually runs. Naturally cold
weather like this gives it all kinds of aches and pains."

Mason proceeded to remove a grease-stained blanket
from the car's hood. "Got to keep it warm in weather like
this. I've got some anti-freeze in 'er, but you never can
tell."

They got in and Mason stepped on the starter. The
motor turned over with a slow protesting moan, caught,

coughed, and roared. The anxious look on Mason's face relaxed into a happy grin. "Ah," he said, adjusting the throttle, "Old Faithful. Cold as she is, she'll respond to my touch—sometimes."

The wheels crunched over the snow and ice. They swung out onto the highway, the motor warmed up, and they began to roll smoothly. The heat from the engine came up in welcome waves. Jack could smell the anti-freeze; somehow it smelled good. He settled back in the seat, warm in a heavy sweater, scarf, and topcoat, and reflected that he had never felt better. His muscles, exercised to the point of exhaustion then heated under a steaming shower, ached pleasantly. His shoulder ached where it had banged into the boards. His back ached when he moved. But there was nothing unpleasant about the aches and the clean tired feeling that reached into every nerve and tendon.

"Boy, I'll really hit the hay tonight," he said.

"Same here," said Mason. "But I've got to do a little work on that math first."

"Math?"

"Yeah, one thing I like to keep up on is math. Math and geometry and subjects like that. We're almost halfway through our junior year now. That means I've got only one year and a half before I go over the river."

"Over the river?" said Jack. "What's over the river? What river?"

Mason grinned. "The Charles River in Boston. You know."

"I know the Charles River. But still you could go over the river to all sorts of places."

"Not me," said Mason, and a determined tone came into his voice, a set look into his good-natured face. His hands seemed to hold the wheel tighter. "I'm headed for the Massachusetts Institute of Technology."

"M.I.T."

"Right," said Mason.

"That's a grind," said Jack.

"You bet it is," said Mason. "That is, in a way it is, but in a way it isn't. If you're interested in science and engineering, it isn't a grind. You're just doing what you want to do most of all, day and night. The stuff interests me—what makes the wheels go round, what makes planes fly. A cousin of mine is an M.I.T. grad. You should hear him. He's been all over, China, South America. Wherever he goes, that degree from M.I.T. opens the doors."

"I suppose so," said Jack.

"It's a fact," said Mason. "They call him in on all kinds of projects—airports, highways, bridges, tunnels. He's down in South America now on a big job. Or maybe it's Central America. I get those places all mixed up. But anyway some government has called him in—and they pay him plenty too."

"I'll bet."

"Sure, plenty," said Mason, taking his foot off the accelerator and pushing the brake pedal. "Hey, look! Here we are at Center and Myrtle. Doc's Place is just down the street. Prob'ly some of the gang there from school. Let's have a hot chocolate, huh?"

"O.K." Jack sat up in the seat. This might be good, he thought. Doc's Place was quite a hangout. All the seniors went there, all the lettermen. Jack had gone there

once or twice and stayed very much in the background, unnoticed. This would be the first time he would go to Doc's Place as a member of the Trent hockey team. He looked through the frosted window of the coupe and saw a cluster of neon lights, a drugstore, a grocery store, then Doc's Place with its pale green neon sign. There was something exciting about that sign, Jack thought.

Mason parked the car and they got out. Jack stamped his feet on the sidewalk, while Mason quickly pulled the blanket over the hood.

"O.K.," said Mason. "That'll keep her tonsils warm." He patted the blanketed engine. "Too bad we can't give you a hot chocolate instead of that nasty ol' anti-freeze." Jack laughed and Mason grinned, his teeth white and even. "Let's go," he said.

Doc's Place was warm and noisy. The juke box was playing, but above it Jack and Mason heard their names called. The voice was Whittemore's. The captain of the Trent team was sitting in a booth, surrounded by other members of the team: Kelly, the goalie, Kuser, the right wing, Levin, the left wing. Heads turned as they made their way toward the booth, heads of envious sophomores, respectful seniors. A bespectacled boy Jack recognized as a senior clapped him on the back and said, "Nice going, Taylor."

"Shove over," said Whittemore. "Make way. Two more hot chocolates, Charley, with lots of marshmallow."

Jack and Mason squeezed into the booth. Jack kept his eyes on Whittemore. Whittemore was the tallest boy on the team, perhaps the best looking, and certainly the best dressed. Jack noticed how often the high school girls at

the soda fountain glanced in his direction. And the boys in the booth hung on his words, that is, all except Mason. Mason didn't seem to care one way or another. Mason just sat there and grinned goodnaturedly. And when Whittemore asked Mason what his first name was, he said, "Jerry," and grinned again.

Jack saw that the booth Whittemore dominated was the noisiest one in Doc's Place and the focal point of attention. Admirers stopped by to pay their respects. "Nice going, gang." "You've got a team there, Dick." "Who's the next victim?"

"The next victim is . . ." Dick Whittemore looked around the booth. "Hey, where's our manager? He was around here a minute ago. Hey, Maloney! Tear yourself away from those women and come over here."

Maloney detached himself from a group of girls at the soda fountain and walked over to the booth. He clicked his heels together and saluted. "Yes, sir," he said.

"At ease, Maloney," said Whittemore. "Produce one of those crumpled papers you cart around in your pockets and tell us who we massacre next."

"I believe it's Jefferson, sir," said Maloney, fishing in his pockets. "Yes, sir, here it is." A crumpled piece of paper emerged. Maloney smoothed it out, read and frowned. "Oh, this isn't it. This is something else."

"What's that?" Whittemore's hand flew out and snatched the paper. "Hey! What is this?" He read aloud: "Agnes 2386, Beulah 8429, Carol 6686-ring 3. Whoops! What a schedule!" The booth rocked with laughter. "Let's see," said Whittemore in a falsetto voice. "We beat Agnes 5-2. Next comes Beulah. How is Beulah, Ma-

ADMIRERS STOPPED BY TO PAY THEIR RESPECTS.

loney?" Now the whole crowd in Doc's Place was roaring.

"Hey, gimme that," cried Maloney, his normally sallow face as red as a ripe strawberry. "I got the wrong list."

"You mean the wrong number," said Jack.

"Yeah," laughed Whittemore, "wrong number."

The crowd laughed. Jack was pleased.

"Aw, come on, Dick," pleaded Maloney.

"You'll get it back, you'll get it back. As soon as my friend Kuser copies down those numbers. After all, you're the manager, Maloney; you're supposed to watch over the welfare of the team and this is certainly the welfare department." Whittemore rested his elbows on the cluttered table.

"Now tell us, Mr. Maloney, what is our schedule, our hockey schedule? Who is our next opponent?"

"Come on, gimme back the list," said Maloney.

"All in good time," said Whittemore.

Maloney grimaced. "O.K." He fished in his pockets and brought forth another piece of paper. The boys in the booth leaned forward.

"Yeah, I was right." Maloney's voice regained some of its self-assurance. "We play Jefferson a week from today at Plaxon's rink. Two weeks from today we play Cooper on the pond, if the pond's frozen. Then Danville. Then City High. The coach gave you fellas the dope this afternoon. There are two really tough games, Cooper and City High."

"What about Jefferson? Are they any good?" said Whittemore.

"Jefferson stinks even on ice," said Maloney, passing off some of his humiliation on the Jefferson hockey team.

"How about Danville?"

Maloney struck a pose beside the booth and his voice took on a sonorous tone. "Let me tell you about Danville. And now, dear listeners, all four million of you, Uncle Dudley's Caramel Cough Syrup, the cough syrup you can use as a hair tonic in the summertime, brings you America's best loved radio commentator, Dr. Elbert Foodlewump. Dr. Foodlewump." Maloney shifted his feet and took his voice up two octaves. "Good evening. And now for the prediction of the week. I preeeeedict that Trent High School will triumph over Danville High by three goals to one, unless Danville scores four goals, in which case Danville will win, unless, of course, there is a tie, in which case, of course . . ." Maloney broke into a fit of coughing. "Please," he gasped, "please, quick, my Uncle Dudley's Caramel Cough Syrup, please. Ah-h-h! No, not on the head, you dope. It's wintertime. In the throat, in the throat. Ah-h-h. And now, good evening, ladies and gentlemen.

Whittemore stopped laughing. "O.K.," he said. "Give the manager back his telephone numbers."

The laughter died away. Doc's Place quieted down. Many groups had left. Whittemore produced a package of cigarettes and then shoved it back in his jacket pocket. He laughed. "I almost forgot. Boy, if there's one game nicotine cuts into, it's ice hockey. Every time I play a game after smoking, I feel knives in my chest. I'll wait till after the Cooper game. Then I'll celebrate and have

one or maybe two." Whittemore pushed back the table. "O.K., men. Charley, what do I owe ya? I do? As much as that? Well, put it on my bill."

Everybody was standing up now.

"Well, so long, Jack. So long, Jerry. See ya at practice."

"So long, Dick."

It had been warm in Doc's Place, Jack thought, warm in more ways than one. He had been taken into the crowd under Whittemore's wing, he had joined the inner circle. The warmth persisted in spite of the cold air outside. It was a cheerful, internal glow.

Mason took the blanket off the car and they got in. Mason stepped on the starter and the engine caught and roared. They swung out into traffic. Jack said, "Whittemore's a swell guy, isn't he?"

"Yeah."

"That's quite a hangout."

"Sure. Doc's Place is O.K."

Jack became silent. He was wondering why Mason did not seem impressed by either Whittemore or Doc's Place. Was he sore about something? Jack thought, The crowd didn't pay as much attention to Mason as they did to me, but then I scored a couple of goals today and Mason didn't. Not that a defenseman is supposed to.

Aloud he said, "Nice little car you got, Jerry."

Mason grinned. "It gets me there. Maybe by the time I get to M.I.T. I'll have something a little better. I'm saving up, working in the summer."

"Good idea," said Jack. No, he thought, Jerry didn't seem sore. He was just thinking about college most of

the time, about M.I.T. Hockey and Doc's Place were all
right, but they didn't seem to matter too much. Maybe
it's better that way, thought Jack.

But he stopped himself. Hockey was a wonderful game.
It was fast and tough and there was no feeling like the
feeling of taking the puck past the other players, eluding
them, outskating them, watching the puck fly into the
nets, dangle and then drop. And Whittemore was a swell
guy, captain of the Trent team, popular, nice-looking, and
a good hockey player. Not as good, though, as the great
Trent player, Nolan. What a player he had been, at Trent
and later at Harvard. What about M.I.T.? Both Harvard
and M.I.T. were over the river, as Jerry said, but M.I.T.
certainly wasn't in the same class as Harvard in athletics.

"Has M.I.T. got a hockey team, Jerry?" Jack asked.

"Darned if I know," said Jerry. "They're not much on
athletics. I guess they just haven't got the time for sports
that other colleges have."

"I guess not," said Jack.

They drove on. They were getting near Jack's home
when Mason said: "You were really hot out there today,
Jack. Two goals. Boy, your line is just about as good as
Whittemore's."

"Not yet," said Jack.

"The coach was certainly pleased," said Mason. "I
could see that, all right."

Yes, thought Jack, Boney Ward had been pleased. All
in all it had been a good day—the game, Doc's Place,
praise from Mason and Whittemore. Whittemore, captain of the Trent team. Maybe next year it would be Tay-

lor, captain of the Trent team. Boy, wouldn't that be
something! To be captain of the team, to be surrounded
by admirers; to go on to Harvard the way Whittemore
probably would, the way Nolan had. To be a great college star—that would be perfect.

THE JEFFERSON HIGH SCHOOL HOCKEY team proved to be almost as bad as Manager Maloney had prophesied. But the Jefferson players were bad in an awkward, encumbering way. They made an obstacle race out of the game. They would fall down, usually in front of an onrushing Trent player, and the fast-skating Trent player would hit the man on the ice, lose his balance, and hurtle into the air. Sometimes the Trent player would describe almost a complete somersault before landing with a painful jarring thud on the hard surface. Sometimes he would fall in a series of jerking, humiliating movements, down first on one knee, then one hip, then one elbow. It was embarrassing and often left the victim with a dull ache in a shoulder or knee. Jefferson hockey sticks seemed to be strewn all over the ice. A Trent skate would step on a Jefferson stick, and the skate would shoot out of control, taking half the skater with it; the other half, trying to catch up, would inevitably bring the player to the ice in a heap. The Trent players swore, Boney Ward was in a fury, and the referee's whistle blew constantly.

The first time Jack got the puck he skated around his

own cage. He heard Kelly, the goalie, say, "Let's see you
go, Jack." He came around the goal skating fast, and
suddenly felt the puck whacked away and sent spinning
toward the boards by a Jefferson player who had lain in
ambush deep in Trent territory, near the narrow corridor
of ice between the cage and backboards where maneuver-
ing is difficult.

Racing for the puck behind the flying skates of the Jefferson player, Jack, irritated and surprised, thought, What
is that guy doing way down here? But the fact remained
that the Jefferson player was down there near the Trent
goal, and now he and Jack were both crashing into the
boards at the side of the rink and slashing at the puck
tangled in their skates. They elbowed and pushed each
other, and the puck became stuck under the Jefferson
player's skate. The referee finally blew his whistle, ending the agony. Now there would be a face-off down in
this dangerous territory near Trent's goal.

It was annoying and humiliating, thought Jack, to lose
the puck before even getting started, to some punk who
skated as if he were angry with the ice and was trying
to trample it underfoot.

The Jefferson forwards skated down for the face-off.
"That's the way, Charlie," they called to their teammate
who had set the trap for Jack. "Nice work, Charlie."

"Watch this, Charlie, you jerk," said Jack under his
breath. His stick flashed down as the puck left the referee's hand, struck the puck, and knocked it forward up
the ice past Charlie. Jack sprang after it with short, chop-
py, speed-gaining strokes of steel against ice. Now he
had the puck and was striking out for the Jefferson goal

with powerful strides, flying over the ice effortlessly. Left far behind was the Jefferson forward line. "Come on, Charlie," said Jack to himself and grinned.

Just ahead now, scrambling, panicky, was the Jefferson defense. Caught too far forward by Jack's quick attack, they saw the danger and began a hasty retreat. Jack was skating fast, faster than any player they had ever encountered. Quickly they skated backwards, their skates weaving. Then they turned with the onrushing player and lashed out with their sticks.

It was too late. Jack had passed them, skating swiftly and serenely, and left them stumbling and waving their sticks ineffectually in the winter air. Now Jack's smoothly developed speed had carried him around the Jefferson defensemen and he was skating in on the Jefferson goalie. It was over in a matter of seconds. The other Jefferson players didn't like to watch because their goalie was helpless and they were responsible for his plight. But they saw the puck fly through the air and they saw one of the goalie's thickly padded legs shoot out. It was too late. The puck was in the nets and the Trent center had scored.

The Jefferson defensemen eyed each other sheepishly. They took care not to look at the Jefferson side of the rink where the Jefferson coach was glaring and chewing gum viciously.

Just then Charlie, their center, who had been a minor hero not too many minutes ago, skated back and said: "What's the matter with you guys? Two of you ought to be able to stop one."

They replied swiftly and savagely, "Oh, yeah? Where were you? Why don't you check back and cover us up?

Who do you think you are, roaming all over the ice, huh?" And other questions, until Charlie took what little dignity he had left and skated toward the referee for the face-off in center ice.

But on other occasions things did not turn out so well for the Trent side. A few minutes later Jack had the puck again and was heading for the Jefferson goal. This time Charlie, the Jefferson center, was checking back in front of his own critical defense. But Jack was skating too fast—Charlie could see that. He wouldn't be able to get near enough to try a pokecheck with his stick. Jack was almost on top of Charlie now, feinting to the left and the right, then flashing by. There was only one thing to do from Charlie's point of view. His stick shot out far and fast, its whole length flat on the ice. Part of it, just the top part of it, slid under the blade of Jack's left skate.

Jack felt the skate that had been cutting sharply into hard ice strike the soft dulling wood. A split second later Jack was skidding along the ice flat on his stomach, and he could hear spectators laughing. Feeling himself fall, he had gone down on one knee and then had slid to the ice. He had learned to become limp, not to yank the body into a wrestling match with the immovable ice, but to break the fall with a padded knee or an outstretched hand. He slid along on his stomach to the skates of the Jefferson defensemen.

One of them jumped over him in hot pursuit of the puck that had been shaken free by Charlie's maneuver. The other grinned down at Jack. This was revenge, revenge for the goal Jack had scored, for the way Jack had blithely skated by a few minutes ago.

"Is your stomach cold?" asked the Jefferson defenseman, grinning.

Jack got up on one knee, got up on both skates, retrieved his stick. Standing firmly on his skates with his stick in his hand, he felt better, sure of himself again, just a little shaken up. He turned on the Jefferson player. "You guys don't know how to play hockey so you stand there and trip, eh?"

"Trip?" mocked the defenseman. "Trip? That's a very naughty word. We don't use it."

Scowling, Jack skated away toward his own goal.

"Come and see us again," called the Jefferson defenseman.

"Don't worry," said Jack over his shoulder.

Jack was sore. He had taken quite a slide on his stomach before the crowd, as pretty a spectacle as a belly-flop off the diving board in the summertime. Moreover, he had lost the puck and the Jefferson players had carried it into dangerous territory. Kelly had had to stop a shot; he dropped the puck to the ice and flipped it out. Then there was an offside pass from Newman to Schwartz and the whistle blew. Jack, thankful that Kelly had stopped the Jefferson shot, skated in for the face-off.

The referee had the whistle in his mouth. He was a rolypoly man with a good-natured pink face. Jack leaned over and spoke to him. "Aren't there any penalties for tripping, ref?"

The referee took his whistle out of his mouth. His pink face became red and it did not look at all good-natured. "When I see 'em," he snarled, "I'll call 'em."

Jack stared down at the ice and did not answer.

A few minutes later there was a mix-up in front of the Jefferson goal. The puck flew this way and that. Players tripped and fell. They piled up in front of the cage, and Jack found himself snarled in a sweaty tangle of hockey players. He untangled himself as the referee's whistle blew.

This isn't hockey, he thought. The beauty, the grace of the game was gone; the clean, fast, open movements, the long dashes, the freedom of lightning movement had degenerated into a sticky, hacking scrimmage.

Between periods Coach Boney Ward agreed. "That's not hockey you're playing out there, fellas. It's shinny, a pick-up game with a bunch of kids. Don't play shinny with those bums. Don't let them make you play their kind of game. That's what they're trying to do. Skate fast and pass," he ordered. "That'll open the game up. Skate down there fast, pass the puck back and forth, make your play, shoot, watch the rebound and then get out of there. Keep your lines together, Whittemore, Taylor. I spoke to the ref about tripping, and he's gonna start handing out penalties. It's about time. But don't play shinny with those bums. We're two goals up now. Make a couple more and we'll call it a day."

The Trent team obeyed. They stopped hacking and steered clear of scrimmages as much as possible. Whittemore and Jack kept their lines together. They skated hard and fast, passed the puck swiftly and surely, opened up the game that had become stuck together by the tactics of the Jefferson players.

Charlie, the roving Jefferson center, tried another ambush near the Trent goal, hoping to pokecheck the puck

away from Jack while hemming him in between the Trent cage and the backboards. Jack swung around his own goal, skating at half speed. Then suddenly he stopped short in a flurry of white ice flakes, reversed his direction, and turned on full speed. Charlie, taken unawares, hopped off in pursuit. Then, seeing the speed Jack had picked up in his smooth powerful rhythm, he gave up in defeat.

Jack had brought the puck up by his own defense a little left of center. Now he was in dead center and skating fast. Ahead of him was a wide open space which Charlie had abandoned to make his ambush. Jack sailed through it. The Jefferson defense converged to meet the attack. Newman and Schwartz coming down on the wings were ready for a pass. Jack held onto the puck until the last minute, drawing the Jefferson defense tight. Then he passed neatly to Newman. Newman took the pass that slithered across the ice, stopped it with the hook of his stick, and skated in on the Jefferson goalie.

The goalie had turned to his right to meet the attack of the Trent left wing now skating in swiftly with the puck. "Shoot," he yelled, in an attempt to rattle Newman. Newman refused to be rattled. He came in closer and closer, dribbling the puck. Then just before it became too late, just before he got within range of the Jefferson goalie's big stick, Newman passed short and straight across the mouth of the Jefferson goal to Schwartz who had closed in from the right. For a split second the round black puck stayed on Schwartz's stick. Then it was off again, to come to rest in the Jefferson nets. The referee's whistle blew to announce Trent's third goal.

Jack, after passing to Newman, had bumped into the

same Jefferson defenseman who had taunted him about the tripping incident. He was standing there now, abashed and openmouthed.

"Hey," said Jack.

The defenseman, still astonished by what had happened, stared back.

"Don't you remember me?" said Jack. "You invited me back—so I came."

The bewildered defenseman turned his mouth down at the corners but said nothing. Jack skated away, grinning.

It wasn't easy to keep the game from becoming one long frenzied scrimmage. Jack's line and Whittemore's line had to skate hard and pass well. But gradually the Jefferson team discovered that ambushing deep in Trent territory left a gap in their own defense which players like Jack and Whittemore could take advantage of. And they soon discovered that tripping didn't pay off, except in penalties. Whittemore's line taught them that lesson.

When the Jefferson forwards brought the puck down the ice, Whittemore pokechecked it free and jumped the Jefferson line. He got away fast, so fast that he left his own wings in the rear. He skated hard and well, not as gracefully or as naturally as Jack, but with determined competence. And he was going fast enough to outmaneuver the Jefferson advance defense. Swinging over to his right, he pulled the Jefferson left defense out of position. The man tried a pokecheck with his stick but Whittemore easily dribbled the puck out of harm's way. The Jefferson defenseman felt the sharp stab of chagrin that comes from swinging clumsily at something that dodges gracefully. Irritated, off balance, he reacted quickly. He twisted the

THE PUCK SKIDDED OVER THE ICE.

hook of his hockey stick and slipped it under one of Whittemore's flashing skates.

Down went Whittemore. Up from the Trent side of the rink came a noisy protest. The referee's whistle blew. His gloved finger pointed squarely at the offending player, his thumb jerked. "Two minutes," he said crisply. The Jefferson defenseman shrugged his shoulders and skated off the rink, followed by jeers from the Trent supporters.

Whittemore got up slowly, brushing white powdered ice off his uniform. He had been jarred by the fall which had landed him on his hip, and he shook his head as if to clear it, then bent over as the referee held the puck for the face-off. The whistle blew, the puck dropped, and Whittemore batted it at the Jefferson goalie. The Jefferson goalie saved and cleared. Kuser, the Trent wing, whacked at the rebound. The Jefferson goalie saved again and sent the puck toward one of his forwards. The puck skidded over the ice. Whittemore, waiting, pounced on it and shot hard, savagely. The puck took the Jefferson goalie by surprise and whistled into the left-hand upper corner of the cage. Goal!

The Trent crowd cheered. "That's the way to do it," said Boney Ward. "Get 'em while they're a man short. Make 'em pay for tripping you, Dick. Attaboy!"

Dick Whittemore made them pay. He kept the pressure on. He led his line down into Jefferson ice as soon as the whistle blew again. Jack could see why Whittemore had been chosen captain. He was a good captain, a good leader. He kept his line in there scrapping, putting on the pressure, taking advantage of the Jefferson penalty. The puck flew at the Jefferson goalie from all angles, low,

high, right, left. The Jefferson goalie stopped it with his hands, his feet, his stick, and his skates, but the inevitable happened. One shot came too fast and Trent had scored another goal. The whistle blew.

"O.K.," said Boney Ward. "That's enough. Get your line in there, Jack. Only three minutes to go. Coast. Take long shots. Take it easy; we got a big game next week."

The final score was Trent 6, Jefferson 1. Coach Boney Ward herded his players into the dressing room. Drinks were brought in—hot chocolate, orangeade. The Trent players sprawled on the long wooden benches, their legs stretched in front of them, their backs slumped against the metal lockers. The warm steamy room smelled of sweat and liniment.

Jack unlaced his skates, pulled them off, and felt the warm blood tingling back into his feet, numb from the tight lacing. He wiped the ice off the blades where it had accumulated and off the hollow aluminum tubes that joined the blades to the leather shoe. Then over each blade he carefully drew an old oily woolen sock. Having placed each skate in a protecting cover, he put his skates out of harm's way in the bottom of his locker.

It pained Jack to see sharp steel skates dropped on a cement floor or to see two naked blades bumped against each other as their owner carelessly held them in one hand.

Jack's skates were oiled regularly, the steel blades, the aluminum tubes, the stout leather itself. Each dent on the hard leather box toe was carefully noted. Skates cost money. Moreover, a player becomes used to a pair of hockey skates, begins to look upon them as part of his

body, begins to feel that he can play in that pair of skates and no other. There wasn't a player on the Trent team who didn't take good care of his skates. When a skate was dropped accidentally and hit a hard object with an ear-ringing clang, the players on the team would wince as if someone had drawn fingernails down a classroom blackboard.

His skates carefully stowed away, Jack reached for the cup of hot chocolate that Manager Maloney held out, leaned back, stretched his aching legs, wriggled his toes in their woolen socks, and relaxed. This was swell, this was the life, they had won again; he had scored two more goals. He was doing well, no doubt about it. He could tell not only by the goals he scored but by Coach Ward's manner toward him. It was Jack this and Jack that. It was no longer Taylor. And the tone of the voice was different, too. At the beginning of the season the tone had been indifferent, almost harsh. It said, "Show me." Now it said, "O.K., you're in. You've shown me and I'm counting on you."

Jack took a big swallow of chocolate. It was so hot it made his eyes water. It burned its way down his throat and warmed his stomach. The warmth spread through him. He finished the chocolate and leaned his head back against the locker. Coach Ward's voice came to him through a pleasant, steamy mist.

"That was better than I thought it was going to be, fellas. Every team has a ragged game in its system and I think we got over ours without doing any harm. Sometimes you get stuck in a game of shinny like you were playing out there in the first period, and before you know

it, the other side, which doesn't know how to skate, is whacking the puck into your goal. Then you go to pieces. You try too hard, you slash and hack. You forget to skate the way you know how, forget to pass, forget to make plays. You're like the duffer on the golf course caught in the sandtrap. You whale away at the puck and nothing happens. You get sore at everybody, including yourself, and you wind up by blowing the game.

Boney Ward paused, a bench scraped, a thick china cup banged into a thick chocolate-stained saucer.

"When you started to play hockey out there today, you played pretty good hockey. I might as well tell you what I think." Boney paused. "I think we've got a good chance at the league championship." Boney's eyes searched the room. "But we've got to play good hockey to win; we've got to beat Cooper and we've got to beat City High." Boney stared at the silent players. "We've got a good chance. You boys are skating well, you're passing well, and you're getting off your shots fast. But don't forget, the real opposition lies ahead. Cooper . . . City High." Boney stuck one foot on the bench and hunched his shoulders. His voice was harsh. "Cooper has one good line, their first line. We have two good lines." Boney's eyes swept Jack and Whittemore. "But—" Boney paused "—Cooper has a tough defense—two brothers, big boys, twins, the Thatcher brothers. They're big and tough. They bodycheck hard. When you come up against them you feel it. It's the best defense we'll meet all year, better than City High, much better than anything you've come up against so far. We won't beat Cooper or City High by any 6-1. We'll be lucky if we win by two goals. But if

get two and they get only one, we're in. And I think we can do it."

Boney dropped one foot off the bench and put his hands in his coat pockets. "I've never seen a defense yet that couldn't be licked, no matter how good it was; and I've seen some good ones in college and pro hockey. But the best defense can be beaten by fast skating and good passing, by keeping your lines together when you attack. A fast skating line that keeps together has an obvious advantage over two defensemen even if they're good. For one thing, it's moving fast and the defense, skating backwards, is moving slower, much slower. For another thing, your fast skating line has three men against your two defensemen. Yes, I know the goalie makes three, but he's in the goal where he belongs. You all know where pay dirt is in hockey—between the two defensemen and the goalie. Get in there, shoot from close up, and the best goalie in the world has the odds stacked against him. Fast skating, good passing, and team play will get you by the Thatcher brothers." Boney dropped his foot off the bench. "And don't forget it."

Getting dressed after taking a shower, Jack found Jerry Mason at his side. "Want a lift, Jack?" There was Jerry's grin, wide and friendly.

"Sure, thanks."

"Hey, fellas! Jack, Jerry." It was Whittemore calling, standing at the door in his tweed jacket and gray flannels, white shirt, red bow tie. "All of you, everybody, over to Doc's Place. The drinks are on me—any nickel drink. Let's go!"

They laughed. They went.

IN THE NEIGHBORHOOD WHERE JACK
lived was a place called Sam's. In the wintertime Sam
hung up a black and white sign that said, "Skates sharpened."

Jack took his skates to Sam the day before the Cooper
game. Sam's shop smelled of oil and leather. The shelves
were lined with shoes and skates. I wonder, thought Jack,
how he can ever tell them apart.

Sam was a short fat man with a gruff voice.

"Hello, Sam," said Jack.

"Hello, young man."

Jack put his skates down on the counter, the blades en-
cased in the oily wool socks.

"I want an extra special skate-sharpening job, Sam."

"Yeah?" Sam's voice was sarcastic. "All my sharpening
is extra special."

"I know, Sam. But I want mine with grooves in the
blades."

"Oh, my gosh," croaked Sam irritably. "Grooves,

grooves, grooves! Now it's grooves. Why do you always want grooves?"

"Look, Sam." Jack took the sock off one skate, exposing the shiny unblemished steel blade. He ran his finger down it lightly. "See this?"

"I see it. I see it."

"It's sharp, isn't it?"

"I dunno. Is it? If it's sharp, why you bring them here?"

Jack's voice was patient. "Because these skates are not sharp enough for the black ice on the pond. I've just tested it. It's black ice, black and like glass, beautiful. You can see your face in it.

"I can see my face in the mirror in the back room," said Sam.

Jack grinned. "O.K. But look, Sam. We've got a big game tomorrow. We play Cooper on the pond and I want my skates super sharp, see? With little grooves running right down the middle of the blade."

"I know what a groove is," said Sam impatiently. He made a face. "Before, you were satisfied with just sharpening. Now it's grooves you want."

"Sure," said Jack. "With grooves I can stop on a dime, just like that!" Jack snapped his fingers. "I can stop just like that, and I can pick up speed just like that and turn on a dime. That's what you need in hockey, Sam. I'm in fast company now."

"Hmm."

"Well, how about it? Can I get 'em tomorrow noon? No later."

"You don't give me much time, young man."

"But the game's tomorrow afternoon at two-thirty."

"Hmm. You don't want much. You come here Friday afternoon. You want your skates in less than twenty-four hours. And you want grooves. You certainly have your nerve, young man."

Jack pleaded. "It's an emergency, Sam. I wouldn't ask if it weren't an emergency. But it's a big game for us. We've got to win this one. And that ice is like glass."

Sam put a pudgy, dirty hand on the skate Jack had unsheathed. "O.K.," he said. "Noon tomorrow. You don't need no check."

A big smile lighted up Jack's face. "Gee, that's swell! Thanks, Sam, thanks a lot."

A T THE APPOINTED HOUR JACK CALLED
for his skates. His heart seemed to beat a little faster when
he opened the door of the shop and saw, not Sam, but a
woman, a round woman with gray hair and sharp eyes.
Jack felt a warning impulse of trouble as he stood before
the counter.

"Is Sam around?" he asked. My voice sounds nervous,
Jack told himself. That's funny. Of course, it's the day of
the Cooper game, but I felt O.K. this morning; in fact,
I felt all right until I came in here and didn't see Sam.

The woman's hands were folded in front of her round
body. She looked at Jack suspiciously. "Sam won't be in
today," she said. "He's not feeling so good."

"Oh," said Jack. He didn't say that he was sorry, because he wasn't thinking of Sam's being sick. He was
thinking anxiously of his skates that were to be sharpened
with grooves. Nervously his eyes roamed around the
crowded shelves.

"You had some skates?" asked the woman.

"Yes," said Jack, tension in his voice.

"Then give me your check," said the woman.

Jack heard the woman say "check," but pretended not to hear. His anxiety to find his skates on the crowded shelves filled his mind. I heard it, thought Jack, I heard her say check, but I'm going to pretend I didn't. Where are my skates, where are they?

The counter was short. The shelves, sagging with shoes and skates, were long. Ignoring the woman, Jack went behind the counter. The skates were stacked one pair beside the other—white skates, black skates, brown skates, plain skates, figure skates, hockey skates. Jack's eyes ran along the top shelf and stopped short on a pair of brown hockey skates—his? No. He shifted to the lower shelf.

"If you'd just give me your check, young man," said the woman and her voice was impatient.

Jack heard the words and again pretended not to hear. His anxious eyes flashed along the lower shelf and fastened on a pair of oily socks. His skates! He bent over quickly and grabbed them. He smiled. "Here they are," he said. He pulled off one sock. The blade was shiny, sharp, and smooth and there was a slight groove in it. They were all ready. Sam must have done them last night before going home. Good old Sam! It was too bad he was sick. What was the woman saying? What was the matter? Was she out of her head?

The woman was angry. Her hand was on Jack's arm. "I am behind the counter, young man, not you. Now where's your check? I give nothing without a check.

Nothing." The woman's voice was loud and determined.

Jack pleaded, "But they're my skates."

"How do I know they're your skates? You come in here, you rush behind my counter. What kind of monkey business is that? You try to take a pair of skates without a check. Maybe I should call a policeman."

If this weren't so serious, thought Jack, it would be funny.

"But Sam . . ." he began.

"Sam is not here," said the woman loudly. "And Sam told me, 'Don't give anything without a check.'"

"Could you call him up?" said Jack desperately.

"We have no phone in this little store," said the woman. "And besides, Sam is in bed upstairs in our house. He can't get up out of a sick bed to come to the phone over a silly matter like a pair of skates."

"Silly!" said Jack indignantly. "It isn't silly. I'm playing in a game today, a big hockey game."

"To me it is silly," said the woman, shrugging her shoulders. "Skating is silly, hockey is sillier. It's a crazy business."

"A lot of people don't think so," said Jack. Then he had an inspiration. "Where does Sam live?"

"In Totham," said the woman, "at 105 Church Street, Totham."

"Totham," repeated Jack and his face fell. Totham was on the other side of Mellton, far beyond the other side of Mellton, near the woolen mills. By streetcar or bus, Totham was an hour's ride, Jack figured. An hour to get there, a search for the house, time to get a note from Sam, an hour back. Two and a half hours, three hours. He had

to be at the clubhouse by the pond at two o'clock sharp. Mason was calling for him. If only he had Mason's car now.

"Look," he said to the woman behind the counter. "My name is Jack Taylor. I play hockey for Trent High School. Today we have a big game. Last night I brought my skates in to Sam. As a special favor he said he'd have 'em ready this morning."

"Maybe that's why Sam is sick," said the woman. "He worked late last night. Maybe on your skates."

Jack stared at the woman. She was immovable. He was tempted to grab his skates from the counter and run. He felt like getting angry. He resisted both impulses. He must somehow reason with this stupid woman.

"If I get a note from Sam," he said, "if the note says give the bearer the skates with the oily socks, would that be O.K.?"

The woman looked at the youth on the other side of the counter. She saw a slight boy of medium height with black hair parted on the side. His eyes, she told herself, were not the eyes of a dishonest boy; they did not shy away, they looked straight at her and pleaded. "O.K.," said the woman. "You get the note from Sam, I give you the skates."

Jack darted out of the shop. He ran down the street into a drugstore and phoned Mason.

Mason's mother answered. "Jerry isn't in," she said. "Is that you, Jack? How are you?"

"I'm fine," said Jack mechanically, and to himself he added, I'm not fine at all, but what of it. What a mess! My only chance of getting to Totham by car is gone.

Mrs. Mason talked on. "And what a lovely day for the game. So nice and clear and cold. I'm sure you boys will win."

I wish I were, said Jack to himself. Aloud he said, "Will Jerry be back soon?"

"No, I don't think so, Jack," said Mrs. Mason. "He had to do several errands for me over in Danville. But he'll be back in time for the game. I'm sure of that. He told me he was going to pick you up."

Jack hung up the receiver with a gesture of despair.

Whittemore, he thought, with a flash of hope. Whittemore might go. What was his number? Jack didn't know. He grabbed the telephone book. What was his father's name? He didn't know that, either. What street did he live on? It was terrible, he thought, how little he knew about Whittemore. And there were so many Whittemores in the phone book. What was the use? He put the phone book back and left the drugstore.

"What a nice day," Mrs. Mason had said. What was nice about it? He walked away along the street and saw a clock in a store window. One o'clock! He hadn't even had lunch. He felt panic-stricken. What would Coach Ward say to this? Would he have another pair of skates? It wasn't likely. And it wouldn't do much good anyway. The skates you're used to, thought Jack, are the skates you need, the exact fit, the right weight. He had to get that note from Sam to convince that woman.

A bus was coming along the street. It would take him into the city towards Totham. The bus stopped and Jack ran for it. It was crowded with women shoppers, people going to the movies. The crowd irritated Jack. And the

bus made slow progress. At every stop female shoppers halted it with frantic waves of stout arms.

The bus crawled, the minutes flew. Another clock in a store window said quarter past one. This was hopeless. Irritated, angry, helpless, Jack pushed to the door and got out. It was no use, he thought. Somewhere or other he would have to find another pair of skates the right size. Maybe the coach would have a pair. But it wouldn't be the same, Jack knew; it wouldn't be any good.

He walked home. The day had turned sour. The clear cold weather had no lift in it; the people on the streets were drab and unfriendly. This had been the day, the big day, the day of the Cooper game. Long, long ago, thought Jack, he had watched Cooper play Trent on the big pond. He had been in grammar school then, learning how to skate. Today he might have been the star. Oh, well, it was hopeless, no use. He would have to go home, force himself to eat something, and wait for Mason. Then they would drive to the pond and give the coach the bad news. If he had only taken the skates somewhere else!

AT THE CLUBHOUSE ON THE SHORE OF the big pond, Coach Ward received the news quietly. The coach had been expecting something to happen to his team, sickness, injury, inelegibility. His eyebrows went up, the corners of his mouth went down. "The skates are in the guy's shop? They're all sharpened and ready to go?"

"Yes, Coach." Jack stared at the clubhouse floor.

"Of all the stupid things I've ever heard!"

"I'm sorry, Coach."

"I don't mean you, Jack." Coach Ward spoke hastily. The boy was upset already, the coach was thinking. If he became too upset he wouldn't be able to play at all "I mean the situation. It's just one of those silly, stupid things that could happen to anyone. Now wait a minute; we'll figure something out. They've got some skates here in the clubhouse. We'll have to do the best we can. I'll get a pair of skates for you and you use those till we get hold of yours. What is this fellow Sam like? Would he give

someone like Maloney a note that would release those skates?"

"I think so," said Jack. His eyes were off the floor now. Coach Ward was in action; there was hope.

"Well, just to make sure, Jack," said the coach, "scribble a note to Sam. Here's a pencil. Here, put it on the back of this card. Tell him the bearer is Tom Maloney. Say this note is from Jack Taylor. Tell him you brought your skates to his shop yesterday. Then put in the part about Maloney, manager of the Trent team. Tell him the woman in the shop won't release the skates without his O.K. So please give Maloney a note saying it's O.K. Wait a minute," added Boney. "How's Maloney going to know your skates?"

"They have oily socks on the blades. Anyway, the woman'll know, all right."

"O.K., put it in the note—skates covered with oily socks. Put it all in, might as well make sure. We want to be sure to get the right skates. O.K. Fine. Hey, Maloney! Get away from those girls and come over here." Maloney hurried over from the clubhouse soda fountain where he had been the center of a group of giggling females.

"Maloney," said Boney Ward, "you have your car here?"

"Yes, sir." Maloney pointed through the clubhouse window to an ancient sedan.

"Oh, that thing," said Boney with contempt, putting one hand in his coat pocket and drawing forth a key ring. "Here, take mine, Maloney."

"Gee, Coach!" Maloney's eyes widened.

"Never mind that, Maloney." Coach Ward glanced at the girls who were watching. "You're going alone, see? This is an emergency."

"Oh," said Maloney.

Boney picked up Jack's note. "Take this note to a guy named Sam Klapnik at 105 Church Street, Totham. And don't go through Mellton. Go around it on the parkway. You ought to make it in fifteen minutes."

"I'll make it in ten," boasted Maloney.

"Not in my car," rasped Boney. "Fifteen. Get Sam to give you a note to that woman in the skate shop near Jack's house, near Harley Street. Jack's skates are the ones covered with oily socks. Bring them here." Coach Ward looked at his wrist watch. "It's now ten past two. Fifteen minutes to Sam's. Leave there by two-thirty. I'll stall the game ten minutes. You can drive by the parkway to the skate shop in twenty minutes. With luck and good head-work you'll be here somewhere in the second period of the game." Coach Ward gave Maloney a friendly whack on the back. "Go!" he commanded.

Jack felt more cheerful. Coach Ward had taken over. Boney's strategy looked promising. Anyway, things were moving. Now the coach was talking to the clubhouse manager about a pair of substitute skates.

Jack tried on the skates Boney had borrowed from the manager. They were size nine. Too small. His toes felt cramped and uncomfortable. He stood up on them and they felt worse. But they would have to do.

"We'll have to stall," said Boney Ward. "I'll put off the start of the game. Then I want you fellas to pass offside, lift the puck over the boards a coupla times. Kick it

around. But play safe. Dick." Boney Ward spoke to
Whittemore, dressed for action in his Trent uniform and
confidently standing on his own skates. "You attack with
your line. Hammer it in there. Jack, I want your line to
play position. Hang on their necks. O.K. Here comes the
ref."

It was a perfect day for the game. The ice was hard and
black and smooth. The cold winter air that nipped at
noses and toes was warmed just enough by the pale sun
hanging in the pale blue sky. The slopes that rolled down
to the big pond were covered with a crusty white snow
sprinkled with green needles from the evergreen trees
that dotted the hills. And the trees themselves, the pines,
spruces, firs, and cedars that had sprinkled green on the
white snow, were themselves sprinkled, decorated with
glistening snowflakes.

A good crowd had turned out for the game, high
school boys and girls, supporters of Trent and Cooper,
and many people who had come to the big pond to skate
and were drawn to the hockey rink by the uniforms and
the cheers. A temporary wooden stand had been built
and its long wooden benches were filled. Reporters were
present. This was a big game, a decisive game. The four
sides of the rectangular rink were black with spectators.
Some stood on their skates; others, without skates, stood
on boards to keep their feet off the ice.

A middle-aged man with ear muffs skated toward the
rink, his skates moving in a steady conservative rhythm
with the skates of the woman in the fur coat beside him.
They moved into a small empty space at the end of the
rink. They heard the hollow scraping sound of the skates

in the rink, saw the uniformed figures—red, white, and blue for Trent; yellow and brown for Cooper.

"This should be a good game," said Ear Muffs.

"Why?" said Fur Coat.

"Because both teams are undefeated. They're both good. They're evenly balanced. Cooper has a good forward line and a strong defense, the Thatcher brothers."

"Are they related to Amos Thatcher?"

"How on earth would I know?" said Ear Muffs.

"Well, sometimes you know a surprising amount of things," said Fur Coat.

"I know what I know," said Ear Muffs, "and don't forget that in my day I played a good deal of hockey. I didn't make the first team at Harvard but I played second string forward and I got my letter." Ear Muffs scraped his skates. The toes of the blades were rounded for figure skating. "What on earth is holding this game up? Oh, here they come. There's Dick Whittemore, the Trent captain."

"He's a nice-looking boy," said Fur Coat.

"Isn't he? Clean cut. Nice lad. He'll be at Harvard next year. He's sure to make the team before he graduates. But what I want to see is this Taylor boy. They tell me he's the boy to watch."

"Who are *they?*" asked Fur Coat.

"Oh, you know," said Ear Muffs impatiently. "People. Shaftesbury Sedgwick, for one."

"Shaftesbury Sedgwick?"

"You know, of Sedgwick, Harrod, and Wigglesby. The big advertising agency. Sedgwick's the chap who took

EAR MUFFS SAW WHITTEMORE GET THE PUCK ON HIS STICK. . . .

Johnny Nolan in tow. You remember Nolan, captain of the Harvard team. Marvelous player. Well, Sedgwick put Nolan through a year at St. Barnes to give him the proper polish; you know, not only for his hockey but for other things. To make him see things the right way."

"What would that be?" said Fur Coat.

"Oh, you know what I mean," said Ear Muffs impatiently. "Nolan came from a no-account family. They were all right, old New England stock, but no-account. Lived in South Boston or some place equally terrible. Well, it was obvious to Shaftesbury Sedgwick that Nolan was destined to be captain of the Harvard hockey team. Well, Sedgwick is a loyal alumnus and a very active one. If Nolan were to be captain of the Harvard team, he had to acquire a certain, ah, a certain, uh, well, you know."

"I suppose so," said Fur Coat.

"Well, anyway," said Ear Muffs, "you see how things worked out. Beautifully. And all of us alumni should be on the watch to see that things always work out that way."

"Naturally," said Fur Coat. "By the way, where is Nolan? What became of him?"

"Nolan? Where is Nolan?" Ear Muffs looked up at the sky as if he expected Nolan to jump out of it. "Oh, yes. Nolan's in the Army or just out of it. He'll probably go back to a cracking good job with Sedgwick, Harrod, and Wigglesby." Ear Muffs grasped the boards in front of him. "Well, at last! There's the face-off. I thought this game would never start.

Ear Muffs saw Whittemore get the puck on his stick and lead his line into action with all the efficiency and

determination that characterized Whittemore's kind of hockey. He circled to get up speed, cutting in front of his own defense with strong strokes of his sharp skates. His handsome face, reddened by the cold, showed tension, the tension of the opening minutes of the game, tension and determination.

His teammates shouted encouragement. Kelly, the goalie, cracked his big goalie stick on the hard ice and called, "Take it down there, Dick!" From the Trent side of the rink came similar calls by voices that were loud and husky with the tension of the moment.

Whittemore got going fast, came up center ice, and passed to Kuser. Kuser, slanting in from left wing, took the puck and evaded the opposing Cooper wing. He passed the puck back to Whittemore as the Cooper defenseman came into the play. Whittemore skated straight for the Cooper defense, then passed to Levin, the right wing. It was a good pass but the Cooper left defense saw it coming. His stick flashed out, deflected the skidding puck, and sent it sliding up the ice to his own left wing. The crowd yelled.

"Aha," said Ear Muffs. "They're on the job, those Thatcher boys. This is going to be a game, yes sir! Two well-matched teams."

Cooper's left wing swooped down on the puck and now the Cooper crowd yelled. Cooper's left wing faked a pass to center and tried to sneak around the Trent defense. Mason stepped into the Cooper wing, hit him hard, and knocked him sprawling, jarring the puck loose. The Trent fans cheered; the Cooper crowd groaned.

"Leave it, leave it!" It was Whittemore, swooping down

from center ice. Mason left it and Whittemore picked it up, circled fast, and started his second attack on the Cooper citadel.

This time Whittemore passed in center ice to Levin, then crossed over to right wing as Levin cut for center. Levin skated in on the Cooper defense and passed out to Whittemore. Whittemore got off a hard shot and the Cooper defenseman, appearing from nowhere, stopped the puck with his shinguards. The puck went "Whock" and fell harmlessly to the ice. The crowd yelled.

"Those Thatcher boys are Johnny on the spot," said Ear Muffs. "Notice how well those boys skate. They all skate remarkably well, they really do. I'm very anxious to see this Taylor boy. They tell me he's a beautiful skater. Oh, look!"

A Cooper wing had succeeded in getting off a shot at the Trent goalie. Kelly caught the flying puck in his left hand, contemptuously dropped it to the ice, shielded it from the piratical stick of a Cooper player, then calmly passed it to Levin, waiting on the right wing.

"Very nice," said Ear Muffs. "Very nice indeed."

Again the determined Trent line attacked, passing back and forth as they skated hard toward the Cooper goal. This time Levin, drawing the Cooper left defense out, passed in to Whittemore at center, and Whittemore dashed for the open door between the Thatcher brothers. The open door closed hard and fast with a thud that reverberated through the pine boards of the rink. Ear Muffs grunted. Fur Coat gasped. Whittemore got up slowly.

"That must have shaken him up," said Ear Muffs. He

wagged his head. "Those Thatcher brothers, oh, my, they hit hard."

"They're brutal," said Fur Coat.

"Oh, no, oh, no," protested Ear Muffs. "It was a perfectly legitimate bodycheck. Whittemore knew what he was doing when he tried to go through the middle. He put his head right in the lion's mouth. It shook him up, no doubt about that."

There was no doubt about it at all; Whittemore was groggy. Mason saw it, got hold of the puck by poke-checking it away from a Cooper wing, and made an off-side pass to Levin. The whistle blew. Coach Boney Ward put his hand on Jack's shoulder. "Take your line out there, Jack, and hold on until Whittemore gets his wind back."

"O.K., Coach."

Jack led his line out toward the referee. His borrowed skates felt awkward and uncomfortable. The Trent cheer that greeted the appearance of his line embarrassed him. He knew that he and his line were going to be a big disappointment. Skating toward the referee, he half tripped, caught himself, and coasted to the face-off. Only when coasting, he thought, did he feel sure of himself.

Jack looked at the referee, and the man looked back as impersonally as referees always seem to look with that whistle stuck in their mouths. Jack stared at the Cooper center and the center's return glance was a mixture of curiosity, awe, and belligerence. He had heard advance stories about Jack's ability. Jack caught the glance and thought, He'll soon find out.

The whistle blew and Jack whacked the puck hap-

hazardly, not caring whether or not he got it, knowing
he could do little with it if he had it. As a result, the
Cooper center got the puck and circled back to get up
speed. Jack skated stiffly into position and waited for the
onslaught. The Cooper center took his time, lined up his
forwards, and then came down the ice skating hard. Jack
braced himself, crouched, waited for the right moment,
and flicked his stick out like a snake's tongue. Crack! His
aim and timing were perfect. The puck tumbled free and
the Cooper center swept by empty-handed, carried forward by his own momentum. The Trent crowd roared.

There was the puck, free, all by itself, begging for a stick
to carry it. Jack started forward fast, the way he always
did when he had the jump on the other line. The clumsy
skates tried to keep up with his agile legs. The blades
skidded on the ice. Jack tripped and fell flat on his stomach. Jeers and laughs came from the Cooper fans. The
Trent supporters stood silent. Newman skated to the rescue, picked up the puck, and continued the attack.

"Great Scott!" said Ear Muffs. "Is that the Taylor boy
I've heard so much about? Good Heavens!"

"He seems awkward, doesn't he?" said Fur Coat.

"Awkward is certainly the word," said Ear Muffs.
"Look at him, how stiff he is."

Jack, his face red, had climbed up on his skates and
was moving slowly and stiffly back toward his own goal.

"Maybe I've got the wrong player," said Ear Muffs.
Turning to the nearest spectator, he asked, "Is that Jack
Taylor out there playing center for Trent?"

The spectator looked at the slight boy of medium
height with the black hair parted on the side and the

face reddened by embarrassment. "Number 8. Yup, that's Taylor. Doesn't seem to be what they say he is, does he?"

"My goodness, no," said Ear Muffs.

Out on the ice, Jack set his jaw and did his best to set his skates. If only I had my own, he thought. If only I hadn't taken them to Sam's. If only Maloney would hurry up.

The puck was at the Cooper end of the rink. Jack was standing five yards in front of his own defense. Mason called up to him, "Are they pretty bad, Jack?"

Jack nodded. They were bad, all right. He felt like a hobbled horse. Lucky thing Newman had come in to take the puck after he had pokechecked it loose. There goes the whistle! Now he would have to skate down into Cooper ice for the face-off. He skated down slowly, carefully. He heard a jeering voice from the Cooper crowd say, "Watch yourself now, Taylor. Don't fall." His face reddened again.

He came to a slow and cautious stop twenty feet out from the Cooper goal. The referee's whistle had untangled a scramble in the corner. Newman could take the face-off. And he did, nicely. Newman snared the puck and sent it slipping over the ice flat and fast to Jack. Jack saw it coming and fear seized him. I'll miss it, he thought.

Crack! The puck struck his stick, forced it back a little, came to a stop. He had it. Now quick, shoot, he told himself. But the borrowed skates moved slowly, stickily, into position. Jack couldn't get set for the shot. He was painfully slow.

The Cooper goalie had plenty of time to change his position and get ready to block the shot. Awkwardly Jack

got off his shot. The puck flew off the ice, kept on flying high and wide, past the goal, over the boards, out of the rink. The referee's whistle blew. Jack heard a voice jeer, "You couldn't hit a barn door, Taylor."

Jack was miserable. His dejection showed in his face, in his slumped shoulders, in his slow, unsteady skates. Ruefully he thought, The coach said to shoot the puck out of the rink, to stall. But he certainly didn't mean to throw away shots like that.

At the side of the rink, Ear Muffs clucked his tongue. "My, my," he said. "What's wrong with that Taylor boy? The goal was wide open."

"Maybe he has stage fright," said Fur Coat.

"Possibly," said Ear Muffs. "There's a big crowd here today and many of them may have come to see him. That might be it. But I must say I'm disappointed. If Taylor continues to stumble around out there, Cooper will win this game."

Cooper was evidently going to make a determined effort to win. When the referee's whistle blew for the face-off that followed Jack's wild shot, Cooper jumped to the attack. The whole Cooper forward line charged ahead. Jack, who had dropped back to center ice, saw the danger and tried to nip the attack in the bud by skating in on it. But his skates refused to give him the necessary speed, and the attack flashed by like a flood flashing by a stranded victim. There was nothing he could do about it. The skates of the Cooper forwards ringing against the hard ice were signals of defeat in Jack's ears. Hopelessly he watched the three Cooper forwards skating down on

his goal. Sick at heart, he saw the outnumbered Trent defense throw itself into the path of the swift attackers. Hoping against hope, he watched the Cooper forwards pass and dribble, pass to the right wing, pass to center, pass to left wing—shot! Nice stop, Kelly! Watch that rebound! Too late! Unguarded, the Cooper center pounced. Whop! Stick against puck. Goal—Cooper!

The whistle blew, the crowd cheered. And over the boards, into the rink, back to the battle, came Captain Whittemore with his first string line.

"Here's Whittemore," said Ear Muffs. "I'll bet that Taylor boy gets a talking-to. He was a complete washout."

"Poor boy, I feel sorry for him," said Fur Coat.

"Pity never helped anyone," said Ear Muffs crisply.

"Maybe not, but . . ." said Fur Coat.

"Watch Whittemore," said Ear Muffs. "Look at the determined expression on his face. He'll try to tie this game up right now."

Ear Muffs was right. Dick Whittemore, refreshed by his rest on the bench, his head clear, his lungs full of cold winter air, went at it hammer and tongs.

The Cooper forward line was tired now, but the Cooper coach didn't dare put in his second string line against Trent's first. Whittemore knew this and attacked relentlessly. He carried the puck down into Cooper territory and he kept it there. The Trent fans howled with delight. Shot after shot bounced off the Cooper goalie's pads. The Cooper forwards were redfaced and panting from chasing Whittemore and his wings up and down the ice. The Thatcher boys were sweating too, but they were still

tough. And they were still forcing the Trent forwards to shoot from far out, a good distance from the Cooper cage, giving the Cooper goalie time to get set.

Then the break came, forced by Whittemore's persistent attack. One of the Thatcher brothers, harassed by the Trent forwards, excited by the hard, bruising play, caught Whittemore's stick savagely, picked it up off the ice with his own stick, jerked it high over his head and used it as a lever to swing Whittemore around and drop him on his knees. The hard hook of Whittemore's stick barely missed another player's eye as it flashed up through the air. Swiftly the referee's whistle blew. His finger pointed firmly at the angry Thatcher boy. His thumb jerked towards the side of the rink. "Two minutes—high sticking."

The Thatcher boy left with angry strokes of his skates. Whittemore got up off his knees, unhurt and eager. This was it. Here was the break he had played for. On the bench, Coach Ward and the Trent players leaned forward tensely. Behind the sideboards Ear Muffs said, "Now watch."

Everybody watched closely. Whittemore crouched for the face-off. The whistle blew, Whittemore pounced, got the puck, and hurled his line forward. A shot bounced off the boards behind the Cooper cage with the crack of a rifle. Whittemore followed it in, wrestled with a Cooper wing, and passed out to Kuser who was waiting in front of the Cooper cage. Kuser shot and the Cooper goalie dropped to his knees and saved. Levin dashed in, picked up the rebound, and slammed it at the goal. Again the Cooper goalie saved. Levin, carried forward by his mo-

mentum, crashed into the goalie, and both players fell to the ice in a heap.

The whistle blew. Face-off again. Whittemore crouched, whacked at the puck, and sent it flying toward Kuser. Kuser knocked it out of the air with his hand, not even feeling the sting in the excitement. He dropped it to the ice, flattened it, and shot low and hard. The Cooper goalie's right leg darted out and the puck hit the thick leather pads, bouncing out right onto the swooping stick of onrushing Dick Whittemore. This time the Cooper goalie was helpless. Kuser's shot had pulled him off balance. Now Whittemore took full advantage of the goalie's plight. He swooped, got the free puck on his stick, and flipped it over the goalie's struggling body into the cage. Goal—Trent!

Ear Muffs thumped the boards with his gloved hands. "Now that," he said hoarsely, "is hockey. Great work, Whittemore, great work!"

"Whittemore is a very determined young man," said Fur Coat.

"Very," agreed Ear Muffs. "They got that goal just in time too, because here comes the other Thatcher brother. It's pretty hard to score when both Thatcher boys are on the ice."

Ear Muffs, Coach Boney Ward, and Whittemore were all agreed on that subject. It was extremely hard to score when the Thatcher boys were both present. But Cooper had no easy time of it either when it took the attack. And the scored stayed 1-1 through the remaining few minutes of the first period and well into the second. And then—

Ear Muffs saw a figure in a white flannel hat and floppy overshoes running across the ice from the clubhouse to the rink, bearing what looked like a pair of hockey skates. He watched the hurrying figure run to the Trent players' bench and he wondered out loud: "Now what on earth? Do they have their skates sharpened during the game? Or did someone's skates come apart?"

"I don't know," said Fur Coat sarcastically.

"Hmmm," said Ear Muffs. "Oh, look! That Taylor boy seems to be putting them on. I wonder if . . . why, of course! It's quite obvious, come to think of it. All that stumbling and falling he did. Of course. He wasn't playing with his own skates."

"But would that make so much difference?" asked Fur Coat.

Ear Muffs looked shocked. "Why, of course," he said. "Absolutely. Why, it could make all the difference in the world." He stared at the Trent bench. "But we'll see."

They saw. So did the other spectators. They saw a skater who made the other players look stiff and awkward and slow. They saw a skater whose body moved effortlessly, so fast, so smoothly that the skates at full flight seemed hardly to touch the ice. They saw a slight boy of medium height who couldn't make an awkward movement if he wanted to, now that he had his own skates. He came dashing out onto the ice of the rink, eager to get into the game.

Ear Muffs watched, fully aware of the drama in the situation. Just the way Jack skated in for the face-off meant something to Ear Muffs, who had once played the

HE WATCHED THE HURRYING FIGURE RUN TO THE TRENT BENCH.

game. "Quite a difference," he said softly. "Quite a difference."

Few others noticed it except Coach Ward and the Trent players. But they all noticed it when the whistle blew and Jack beat the Cooper center to the puck and circled back to build up speed. Then they noticed it, they couldn't fail to notice it—the grace and the beauty and the speed, speed to spare. They watched Jack's skates flash, noticed his legs move, watched his body fly over the ice. Collectively they let out a long low "Ah-h-h" of admiration.

"Ah-h-h," said Ear Muffs with the others. "I was right, I was right. Look at that boy skate!"

Jack wound up in a flashing semicircle. He swept up the ice in front of his own defense and Mason urged him on in a hoarse, excited voice, "Show 'em!" he cried. "Show 'em, Jack boy!"

Jack was going like a whirlwind when he reached center ice. The Cooper forward line stood dazed by this display of speed. They saw a red-white-and-blue blur coming toward them; their mouths dropped open. They lashed out with their sticks, scrambled on their skates; too late, the blur was past. Down on the Cooper defense it flew. The Thatcher brothers gaped, then threw their big bodies into action. But the blur was around them in a flash, in front of the Cooper goal, shooting. The Cooper goalie hurled himself forward and saved magnificently. The crowd that had worked itself up to a crescendo of noise as Jack hurtled down the ice exploded in a cheer for the goalie.

Jack saw the puck plunge into the goalie's pads as he

leaped over the prostrate goalie and turned sharply to cut
back up the ice. The crowd had settled down, thinking
the play finished. The goalie had cleared the puck to one
of the Thatcher brothers. The big Thatcher boy lumbered
up the ice all by himself. Jack flew after him. It was like
a fleet fighter plane flashing after a clumsy bomber.

The crowd, catching up with the action, saw what was
going to happen and began to roar again. Jack swooped
down on the Thatcher brother. The boy looked over his
shoulder, saw what was coming, jerked into action. But
Jack had already skidded down on one knee and laid his
hockey stick almost flat on the ice. Curving its hook
around the Thatcher boy's stick, he deftly stole the puck
away. The crowd let out a roar. There was Thatcher,
stopping sharp and turning and hopping frantically after
a fleet shadow that was already out of reach. Now the
other Thatcher boy was left alone to defend the goal. He
dug his skates hard into the ice, stared at the meteor flashing his way, and lunged at it viciously. He missed by
several feet, tripped, stumbled, sprawled. From a reclin-
ing position on the frozen surface of the rink, he watched
Jack pull the Cooper goalie out of the nets with a quick
feint and whang the puck into the empty cage. Goal—
Trent! Score: Trent 2, Cooper 1.

The crowd went wild. Coach Boney Ward pounded
Dick Whittemore, Dick Whittemore pounded Boney
Ward. Ear Muffs whacked an astonished Fur Coat on the
back, and shouted, "I thought so! Shades of Johnny
Nolan!"

. . . . .

THE NEXT DAY'S PAPERS TOLD THE STORY.
The high school sports reporter for the *World-Journal*
wrote: "In a game with the last minute twist of a Hollywood thriller, Trent High trimmed Cooper yesterday in
a hockey game played on the fast black ice of the big
pond. Under a cold blue sky that turned a big crowd's
cheers into steam, Jack Taylor, Trent's second-string
center, showed skating and stick-handling that recalled
the famous Trent star, Johnny Nolan, who went on from
Trent to become a celebrated captain of the Harvard team
and later still a captain in the U. S. Army.

"The twist that brought victory to Trent was revealed
when Coach Boney Ward informed the press that his
star, Jack Taylor, had played part of the game on borrowed skates which severely cramped his style. The truth
of Ward's story was reinforced by Taylor's performance
when his own skates arrived in the second period, having
been rescued from a skate shop by Trent Manager Maloney. On his own skates Taylor was a different player,

so different in fact that Cooper was dazed by his speed
and the puck was soon in the Cooper cage, after two bril-
liant solo dashes by Jack, one of which missed by inches
and the second of which gave Trent what proved to be
the winning goal."

Mason whistled and tossed the newspaper into Jack's
lap. "Star it says, right there in print."

They were sitting in Mason's coupe outside a stationery
store in Mellton. Mason grinned at Jack's red face.
"What's the matter? You've gotta get used to this, Jack.
You made people think of Johnny Nolan."

"Aw, cut it out."

"Me cut it out?" Mason feigned indignation. "What the
heck have I got to do with it? The paper said it, not me."

Jack folded the paper. "Johnny Nolan," he said slowly.
"Gee, I saw him play on the pond five, six years ago."

"I saw him play once for Harvard," said Mason. "He
was terrific."

"So he was in the Army," said Jack, as if to himself.

"I wonder if we'd recognize him now if we saw him,"
said Mason.

"I bet I would," said Jack. "He was pretty tall and sort
of thin, and he carried himself in a certain way. Y' know,
when I was eleven years old I thought Johnny Nolan
was a sort of superman."

"Sure," said Mason. "And now you're a superman to
some eleven-year-old."

"D'ya really think so?" said Jack.

"Why not?" said Mason. "Hero worship." He stepped
on the starter. "Let's go. We told Whittemore we'd be at
his house by two. Do you ever think, Jack," said Mason,

twisting the coupe away from the curb, "that a month ago Dick Whittemore and the bigshots at Trent didn't even know a couple of guys named Mason and Taylor?"

"Yeah," said Jack. "We're in with the crowd now, all right."

"We certainly are, maybe too much so," said Mason. "I haven't cracked a book in a week, and if I don't start pulling my math marks up, my old man is going to land on me like a ton of bricks. Don't forget, Jack, your math has to be pretty good to get you into M.I.T."

"I suppose so."

Mason braked for a red light, shifted into neutral, and pumped the accelerator. "You have to keep jabbing this engine all the time or it'll stall," he said, peering up at the traffic light. "Good old gasoline engines. I wonder how much longer we'll be depending on these things."

The light changed and Mason sent the coupe forward. "Look at these jet propulsion planes that use kerosene. Imagine that, Jack, kerosene. And when we get the atomic engine, oh, boy!" Mason's voice vibrated with enthusiasm. "Think of all we're gonna see in the next ten or twenty or thirty years. Things you and I wouldn't have dreamed of a few years ago. And if I get into M.I.T., I'm gonna have a ringside seat." Mason paused. "How about it, Jack?"

"How about what?"

"How about going to M.I.T. with me? You're good at math and physics. Think of it—jet propulsion, atomic energy—all that sort of stuff right here under our noses."

"Yeah, but . . ."

"I know, I know. No one ever heard of their hockey

team. So what? Once you get wrapped around a few atoms, you'll have something a million times as exciting as hockey. Come on, Jack."

"Wait a minute." Jack grinned. "We don't have to sign up right now, do we?"

"I wish I could," said Mason. "Anyway, keep thinking about it, will ya?"

"Sure," said Jack. And he thought to himself, Mason's right. Big things are going to happen, have happened already. It's going to be something to see, wonderful to be part of. But there was no hurry. It didn't mean he had to stop playing hockey right now. Why, he was just coming into his own. He was a star; the papers said so.

The papers went on to say a week later that Trent beat Danville in a one-sided and unexciting game. Then the sportswriters turned to something they could really write about—the coming conflict between Trent and City High. This game, the papers announced, would bring together two undefeated teams. The winner would automatically become the metropolitan champion. And because of the importance of the game and the size of the audience and uncertain weather conditions, the game would be played on the indoor rink of the Boston Garden.

For now it was late in the season. The ice on the big pond was soft and mushy. Even at Plaxon's rink the ice was melting. Spring was just around the corner. New England was going through that drab and draughty period when neither winter nor spring controls the skies; when the white snow loses its beauty and the buds on the trees threaten to burst.

The Boston Garden is a replica of New York's Madison

Square Garden. It is an enormous cave with tiers and tiers of seats stretching up from the white ice of the big rink, up and up, higher and higher, to the dizzy altitudes near the tremendous roof. It is so vast an amphitheater that the average athlete feels awed by his first appearance on its stage.

Jack did not feel that way. Actually, he felt a little depressed. "It's sort of gloomy, isn't it?" he said to Mason as they paused, two small figures at the opening of the long dark cement tunnel that leads from the arena to the dressing rooms.

"Yeah, Smells sort of stale in here," said Mason. "As if someone had left some old cigars under the seats. But look at that ice, as smooth and white as the frosting on a cake."

"Yeah, slick. But still I think I'd rather play outdoors. I like fresh air."

Jack couldn't figure out why, but he knew that the old excitement was missing; the old thrill he used to feel before a game; the nervous tension as he saw the crowd gather, as he approached the rink in the flattering knowledge that he was one of the players the crowd had come to see, a member of the Trent team.

"Harvard plays most of its games here," Mason was saying.

"I know," said Jack. He thought, if I go to Harvard, if I make the team as they say I will, I'll be playing and practicing here regularly. And somehow or other that didn't seem as wonderful as it had seemed a month ago. Had Mason said that on purpose to point something out to him? He glanced at Mason's face as they walked through the tunnel. In the gray light of the tunnel he

couldn't tell. Good old Mason, he thought, Mason and
M.I.T. He remembered Mason's words: "No one ever
heard of their hockey team." And if I play hockey at
Harvard, this is where I'll play. Here in this enormous
place, so violently different from the outdoor rinks. Do I
really want to, Jack thought suddenly.

But in the dressing room some of the old feeling came
back with the warm words of greeting from Coach Ward
and Dick Whittemore and the other members of the team.
Here, Jack felt, were good friends. Their cries of welcome, their slaps on the back, said, "Here's the star, the
best player on the team, the man who will beat City High
for us, who will win the championship for us."

Coach Boney Ward was talking, standing in his familiar pose with one foot on a bench, one elbow resting
on a chunky thigh. Here was the familiar voice, the familiar rasp. But the tone was much more confidential.
Boney knew his team now; it had proved itself, he was
proud of it, and his tone showed it. "Well," said Coach
Ward, "I suppose you all remember that speech I made
after our first game when I said that we had a chance for
the championship. Well"—one foot dropped to the floor,
the other foot rose to the bench—"here we are, fellas. The
last game of the season—City High. And we're undefeated. You looked good against Danville but Danville
was a pushover; you know that as well as I do. They're
not in the same class as City High. I know how you feel.
You feel that you're a good team. You are. We won't kid
about that. But overconfidence will beat any team, no
matter how good. Don't let it beat you. You're playing
in the Garden; it's a big place. Some of you," Boney

glanced at Jack and Whittemore, "will probably be playing here for many years to come. Don't let the Garden
scare you; don't let the big crowd rattle you. Go out there
and get goals." The foot dropped to the dressing-room
floor, the hands went into the pockets. "And get me that
championship!"

Jack sat on the bench and watched Whittemore's line
take the ice. He listened to the familiar scraping sound
of the skates, listened to the cheers of the big crowd echo-
ing, reverberating in the enormous cave. Jack felt the old
pre-game tension return as the two forward lines crouched
for the face-off. The City High players in orange and
black uniforms looked as if they could play good hockey,
and their record of five victories and no defeats was just
as good as Trent's.

This was the big game, as Boney Ward had predicted,
as the morning papers had announced, as the roaring of
the big crowd proved. The location of the game proved
it too—the Garden with its professional equipment, the
little gate in the boards that swung open to let the players
out on the ice, the electric lights behind the cages that
flashed red when a goal was scored; and the wonderful
artificial ice laid over a network of pipes, white, slick,
smooth. How would it be, Jack asked himself, to skate
out on that ice as a member of the Harvard team, to hear
thousands of hockey fans cheering, college students and
their pretty girls, cheering, calling his name as he dashed
down the ice?

The referee's whistle broke his reverie. The championship game had started. Whittemore's stick swooped and
the puck tumbled back to Kuser. With no preliminaries

Kuser skated straight ahead. City High's right wing retreated, pokechecked, knocked the puck free. The City
High line jumped and attacked, three good skaters heading for the Trent goal, a scoring play in the making. The
City crowd yelled. But Whittemore, seeing the danger,
skidded to a stop, reversed his direction, and skated at
full speed between the City wings. He broke up the play,
batting the puck off a city player's stick, sliding it in
front of him, taking it far down the ice behind his own
cage. The Trent fans cheered, "Yea, Whittemore!"

Whittemore reformed his line. Once more he led it
down the ice. The City forwards checked back effi-
ciently, skating in front of the oncoming Trent forwards,
watching for an opportunity to pokecheck. The opportunity came when Levin sent a short pass to Whittemore
and Whittemore got a little too close to the City center.
The latter's stick came down with a smack and the puck
went spinning—City had broken up the Trent attack.
City got the puck, jumped, passed. The whistle blew—
City offside.

Three minutes of the first period had elapsed. Boney
Ward put his hand on Jack's shoulder. It was a friendly
hand, not a claw. "O.K., Jack go out there and get me
one goal, just one goal."

Jack smiled. "I'll try," he said.

Manager Maloney opened the little gate in the boards
and slapped Jack on the back. "Give 'em the old one-
two," he said.

He led his line out on the ice. Dick Whittemore, perspiring, panting, clapped Jack on the back as he skated
off. "Let's see you go, Jack."

JACK SAW THE BLACK PUCK JUST BEFORE IT HIT THE BACKBOARDS.

Jack grinned. He felt sure of himself. His skates felt snug, the blades sharp and grooved. Newman and Schwartz were close by. Mason was chanting, "Here we go, here we go." Kelly, the goalie, was talking it up, and the Trent fans yelled, "Yea, Taylor!" It was quite a reception.

Jack felt his hands grow moist inside the big leather gauntlets. He glanced at the City center. So City was leaving its first string line in. He looked up at the referee, and for the first time he noticed an expression on what was usually an expressionless face. The referee was looking at him and there was curiosity in the look. He seemed to be saying, "So this is Jack Taylor."

The whistle blew short and sharp, the puck dropped, the sticks cracked. The puck flew up in the air, dropped to the ice, and rolled toward City's right wing. The City wing skated back toward his own goal, taking his time. Jack skated over to Newman and said, "When we get it, let's try that X play."

"O.K.," said Newman.

Jack repeated the suggestion to Schwartz and then skated back to center ice a few seconds before the arrival of the City forwards. Jack and his forward line had worked out the X play in their last practice session at Plaxon's rink. It was based on a decoy move by Jack. City High, Jack thought, looked ripe for the X play.

City was taking its time bringing the puck up the ice. The City right wing had it, then passed it over to the center, and the City center seemed to be skating at half-speed as he approached center ice. Then Jack saw why. Just before the City center got within range of Jack's

stick, he let go with a shot, a long high shot that went sailing down the ice pursued by the whole City forward line that had suddenly turned on all its speed. Turning, Jack saw the black puck just before it hit the backboards, heard it whack into the boards, saw it bounce back out in front of the Trent goal and perilously near it. The whole City line, skating at top speed, was swooping down on it. The City left wing had it; he was shooting. Kelly, the Trent goalie, saved in the nick of time. The puck bounced out, this time off Kelly's wide leather pads. It flashed past the scrambling Trent defense. The City center was on it. Jack, coming up fast, hooked out with his stick. Too late!

The City center got off his shot; the flying puck caught Kelly off balance and flew past the goalie. The red light flashed! Goal—City High! A great roar went up from the crowd, a roar that echoed and re-echoed throughout the vast arena.

Angry with himself, Jack skated to center ice for the face-off. It was all my fault, he told himself. He had been beaten at the face-off, had chatted casually and confidently about making a play, had been caught completely off guard, had let City's center bat in a rebound. Coach Boney Ward had been dead right—overconfidence. Now they had spotted City High a goal and City High was a smooth-working, undefeated team that knew how to play hockey, smart hockey. Jack knew that his line's playing time was almost up. It was almost time for Whittemore to come back in, and the score, instead of being 1-0 in favor of Trent as Coach Boney Ward had planned, was 1-0 in favor of City High.

Jack knew his face must show his chagrin. He knew the crowd was looking at him now and probably saying to itself, "For a player with his build-up, this Taylor isn't so hot."

Newman and Schwartz skated in close and Jack said, "It's still the X play. Let's get one quick." They nodded and skated to their positions. Jack glided in for the face-off and felt the referee's eyes looking him over as if to say. "You didn't look so good on that one, Taylor."

The whistle blew and Jack trapped the puck and sneaked it away. He circled to get up speed, his legs pumping under him like two well-oiled pistons. The crowd could see his speed now. They drew in their breaths and a kind of odd, low murmur rose from their throats.

Kelly, the Trent goalie, whacked his big stick on the ice and Mason yelled, "Go get 'em, Jack," as he whistled by.

Jack was going fast as he cut his semicircle, one skate in front of the other. His legs and arms were blended into a smooth-running engine that kept pumping more speed into its cylinders. By the time he hit center ice, Jack was skating at a speed that had the crowd standing up and shouting. Then he was over into City territory, flashing past the City forward line, weaving skillfully between the City center and the City right wing, making them look awkward and helpless with his graceful speed. Now he was flying down deep into City ice, a little over to the left with the City defense beginning to scramble, concentrating on him, fascinated by his speed and the danger it represented. One City player was scuffling along

with him, hacking and chopping; the other hesitated between Jack and the goal with indecisive movements.

The cry of the crowd was rising, rising to a roar as Jack skirted the City defense, pulling it over with him to the left, farther over, deeper, until the City goal was clear. Then, too late, the City defense saw the pass flying flat from Jack's stick, swiftly and surely to Newman ten feet behind and to the right. The black puck clung to Newman's stick for no more than a second, then skidded over to Schwartz, who crouched free and all alone in front of the City goal. In the split second before Schwartz got off his shot, the City defense man nearest the goal saw what was going to happen and tried to throw himself back into the play. Simultaneously the City goalie, who had been watching Jack, expecting a shot at any second, tried to swing around to face the new peril. Both efforts were too late.

Schwartz shot. The puck flew through the air and into the cage. The red light flashed, the crowd roared. Goal—Trent! Score 1-1. The cheers of the crowd rose to the Garden rafters.

Jack skated over and slapped his wings on their shoulders. The X play had worked. And just in time, for the little gate in front of the Trent bench was opening and Whittemore was leading his line out onto the ice.

Captain Whittemore's line played for the rest of the period. Neither side scored, and the period ended with one goal for Trent and one goal for City High. But Boney Ward was content. By using Jack Taylor as a scoring threat, he had forced City High to use its first string line

during the entire first period. Boney knew well how tired
lungs and legs could become, skating at full tilt with no
pause for rest, pursuing and being pursued in the exhaust-
ing game of attack and counterattack that is ice hockey.

This was the championship, this was the last game
Captain Dick Whittemore would play for Trent, and it
would certainly be fitting and proper for Captain Whittemore to play as much of the game as possible. If anyone
could wear down an opponent, it was Dick Whittemore
with his persistent, punishing attack. Boney Ward saw
signs of wear and tear already in the City High team.
Another period and it would begin to fall apart. If Captain Whittemore fell apart at the same time, well, thought
Boney, that would be just too bad, the fortunes of war
and sport. For when the break-up occurred, there was
Jack Taylor ready, willing, and most certainly able to go
in there and break the game wide open. This would happen, Boney predicted to himself, in the third period.

Coach Boney Ward was a good prophet. The second
period of the game proceeded as prophesied. Captain
Whittemore attacked and pursued, attacked and pursued,
until City High was red-faced and panting. Trent scored
another goal; so did City High. Jack's line went in for
three minutes but played it safe, according to husky in-
structions from Coach Ward. Then came the third and
final period.

Boney Ward leaned over and put a friendly hand on
Dick Whittemore's shoulder. "I'm gonna let Jack start this
period, Dick. Give you a rest, see?"

Whittemore turned on his coach. Listening, watching,

Jack saw the hurt in Whittemore's eyes, the surprise, the indignation. "But, Coach, this is my last game for Trent. I've got 'em groggy out there now."

"Sure you have, Dick, old boy," said Boney Ward. "You've got 'em just where we want 'em. Now we throw in a fresh line, see? I'll put you back in after you get a rest."

Whittemore turned away and stared at the floor. Jack thought, This is pretty tough on Dick; after all it's his last game. Jack spoke up. "Look, Coach . . ."

Boney Ward swung around. There was anger in his eyes and in the thin line of his mouth. "Shut up! I'm running this team. Not you, or Whittemore either. I want that championship. And we're gonna get it." Boney Ward poured syrup in his voice, softened his expression. "Now look, fellas. I've been pretty square with you all season. We've worked pretty well together. I've made this team out of a bunch of rookies. My strategy's worked every time. And it's going to work this time too. Now go out there, Taylor, and start making that red light flash."

Jack felt Boney's hand on his shoulder. It was a claw that bit into bone and flesh. He gave his shoulder a violent wrench and threw the hand off. Then he stepped through the gate and led his line out onto the ice. The Trent fans rose and cheered. Last game. Last period. "Come on, Jack! Put it in the bag. Come on-n-n, Taylor!"

It was a rousing cheer, but it didn't take away the bad taste from Jack's mouth, the bad taste that had seemed to creep in when he first saw the inside of the Garden, that had grown worse during the recent scene on the bench. As he skated toward center ice, Jack thought that

he didn't like Boney Ward, he didn't like the drab com-
mercial atmosphere of the Garden, he didn't like hurt-
ing the feelings of a good guy like Whittemore—just to
be sure to win a hockey game. Of course, it was a championship game but . . .

The whistle interrupted his chain of thought. He swung
half-heartedly at the puck and was not surprised when
the City High center stole it away from him. City High
attacked, its center carrying the puck, and Jack let the
center get by when he missed a listless pokecheck. The
City High forward line surged on the Trent goal and the
Trent defense had to scramble. The City center got off a
hard shot and Kelly saved. City's right wing skated in
fast, picked up the rebound, and whacked it at the Trent
cage. Kelly dived and made a wonderful save and the
crowd let out a yell. The whistle blew and the referee ex-
tracted the puck from under the prostrate Trent goalie.

Mason skated up to Jack and said, "Come on, Jack!
Let's go!"

"Yeah," said Jack.

The whistle blew and Newman broke free with the
puck. Jack skated along with him, took a pass, and
reached center ice. He heard the crowd yell as he got the
puck, and he knew what they wanted. They wanted to
see him cut loose with all his speed. But the bad taste was
still in his mouth and, like a poison, it seemed to be af-
fecting his legs. So at center ice, with the crowd yelling
for him to open up, he passed the puck over to Schwartz.
The yelling died out as Schwartz skated in methodically
and took a methodical shot, while Newman tried for the
rebound and missed. Jack found himself bodychecked

out of the play by a determined City player. He did not resist.

City got the puck and brought it up the ice and Jack checked back languidly. As a result, the City center got through again and once more the Trent defense had to scramble. Mason stepped in front of the City center and knocked him sprawling with a hard bodycheck. Then Mason made a desperate lunge for City's right wing and pokechecked the puck free as the wing was about to shoot for the Trent goal. It was a nice piece of defensive play and the crowd gave Mason a cheer. But he didn't hear it. With the City attack stopped, he had turned his attention to Jack and his voice was low and angry "Listen, Jack! For gosh sake, give us a hand!"

The angry expression on Mason's usually goodnatured face, the look of reproof, shook Jack much more than the bodycheck he had just suffered from the City defense. It brought him out of the depressing circle of thoughts that had been spinning in his mind—thoughts about the Garden and Whittemore and Boney Ward. He remembered now that his good friend, Mason, was on the same team, fighting furiously to win this championship game, playing as hard as he could to cover his own position and the gaps that Jack's lethargy created in the Trent defense. Mason doesn't care as much about hockey as I do, thought Jack, but when he decides to do something he sees it through. I can't let Mason down. The thought seemed to send a message down through the muscles of his legs to his skates, a message that was answered by his speed that took him in a matter of seconds

to the puck that lay loose near the backboards, got him there a split second ahead of the City High wing.

It was a different Taylor now and the crowd, sensing the change, let out that curious growling murmur that rises in direct ratio to the speed of the attacking skater. Jack circled his own cage, his skates cutting into the ice sharp and sure, making a thrilling rhythmic sound that echoed in the vast spaces of the amphitheater. Kelly, the goalie, could see that this was going to be something to watch and he turned his head to follow Jack's swift dash around the Trent cage, calling out to him hoarsely as he sped by, "Let's see you take it down there, Jack boy."

Jack came around his own cage at a speed that had the gallery gasping. A City wing, who had lurked near the Trent cage, found himself stabbing at a phantom figure. The figure swerved swiftly, crossed over into center ice, its stick smoothly dribbling the puck, and outsped the two City wings who lashed out futilely. Jack swept down on the City defense with the crowd in an uproar. He slipped the black puck deftly between the two City defensemen, who crunched together to prevent a dash between them, and found to their horror that Jack had suddenly ducked around them. He picked up the puck which he had slid between their frantic, stumbling skates and all at once was in on their unprotected goalie. The crowd, exploding into a roar of surprise and admiration, saw for just one thrilling second the pattern of the perfect play—Jack with the puck between the two gaping defensemen and the goal. Then the picture blurred. The goalie dived desperately. Jack dribbled the puck out of

reach, swerved, and backhanded it into the cage. The red light flashed triumphantly while the crowd thundered its tribute. The score was Trent 3, City High 2.

The tense expression that had been on Boney Ward's face vanished. He relaxed, his thin lips lost their anger, his claws once more became hands. His face, split by a toothy smile, was almost beatific in its happiness. He leaned over and placed a friendly hand, a gentle soothing hand, on the slumped shoulder of Captain Richard Witte-more.

"We got it, Dick," he purred. "Strategy pays rich dividends. Don't fret, fella. You'll be back in there in jig time, just as soon's you get your wind back."

Whittemore remained silent, staring at the floor.

Sour grapes, said Boney to himself, looking at his captain. Jealousy. Suppose it is his last game! We gotta win the championship, don't we? He shifted his gaze and fastened it on Jack, coming up the ice. Boy, that kid can skate; a natural, the kind that crowds love. Nice stickhandler, too. Doesn't have the hardest shot in the league, but hard enough. And anyway, when you get in as close to the other guy's goal as Taylor can, all you need is a flip and the puck is in. What a player! And one more year at Trent, too! That should be a pip. Just the kind of a player the crowd laps up, fast as lightning, graceful; solo stuff and the timing—perfect. Whenever the chips are down, you can count on the kid; a money player. Money, hmm, plenty of it in a player like that. And one more season at Trent. Boy!

Boney rubbed his dry hands in delight. Just the right build-up this year. Next year the sockeroo. Plenty of pic-

JACK SWERVED AND BACKHANDED THE PUCK INTO THE CAGE.

tures in all the papers. "Jack Taylor, high school sensation, with his great coach, the developer of champions, Boney Ward." "How I developed the High School sensation, Jack Taylor. From a clumsy rookie to a star," or something along those lines. But that wasn't all. Get him a try-out with a minor league team, then on to the pros, the Boston Bruins or the New York Rangers—to the highest bidder! Boy! An ironclad contract signed with his family's approval. A nice piece of the kid's pro salary. How the pro league would go for a good American player instead of all those Canucks! It looked good, it looked great. Publicity, fame—and dough. With this happy dream in front of his canny eyes, Boney Ward watched his star get set for the face-off.

Jack beat his opponent to the puck, swirled around the ice in a graceful arc, and led his forward line into City territory. There he swerved sharply past the City center and flipped a perfect pass to Newman as he swept down on the City defensemen. Dodging a bodycheck, Jack took a good pass back from Newman, darted around the right side of the City cage, and popped up like a jack-in-the-box on the other side. Then he faked a pass out to Schwartz and, with the quick strike of a rattler, hammered the puck into the small opening between the goalie's leg pads and the cage.

Boney Ward shouted and jumped to his feet, pounding the boards in front of his barrel-like body. He could feel that championship suddenly drop in his pocket, see the future bright and shiny with fame and money.

This time the newspaper stories about the game were extravagant enough to send waves of excitement through

the classrooms of Trent High School. There were long
stories about Trent winning the championship, a picture
of the team, a close-up of Boney Ward, and a big picture
of Jack Taylor taken under a photographer's flash bulb
on the ice in a face-off pose. There was another story a
day later, smaller, to be sure, but a good story nevertheless.
It said: "Jack Taylor elected captain of next year's Trent
team. Trent star logical choice, says Boney Ward."

It was a wonderful wind-up to an exciting season. Jack's
appearance with Mason in Doc's Place was the signal for
loud and flattering cries of welcome. Even Jerry was impressed by the noise and the popularity.

It lasted for almost a week. Then the bottom suddenly
dropped out as suddenly as the ice had melted on the
pond, leaving in its place gentle, wind-rippled, quiet
water. Gone with unbelievable speed were the ice, the
hockey rink, the cheering crowds. Gone too was the cor-
diality of the welcome at Doc's Place. Now the center
table was exclusively for seniors unless, of course, you
happened to be a baseball star. Jack was not a baseball
star. Neither was Mason. The ice had melted.

The excitement and happiness that had accompanied
the cheers of an admiring crowd and his election as captain of the Trent hockey team seemed to have faded completely from Jack's life. There had been one last hockey
party at Dick Whittemore's, at which Boney Ward had
given out the dark blue sweaters with the big red T's for
Trent. And Whittemore had been as cordial and friendly
as ever, despite the incident at the Garden. In fact, the
incident had blurred in Jack's memory after the excitement of winning the championship and all the stories and

pictures in the papers. He remembered that Boney had put Whittemore back just a couple of minutes before the final whistle blew. By that time, of course, the game was in the bag.

Well, that had been the last invitation from Dick Whittemore. The parties at his house were now attended by older friends in the senior class and baseball players. At Doc's Place greetings were still given to people like Mason and Jack, but the old effusiveness was gone. Just the other day, Jack remembered, that bright and cheerful ladies' man, Maloney, had answered a cordial slap on the back with a rather distant, "Oh, hello, Jack." It was almost as if he said, "Why do you hang around, now the hockey season's over?"

NOW IT WAS SPRING, WARM, SWEET-smelling. But there was no beauty in it, Jack thought. He didn't notice the songs of the robins, the wonderful smell of the fresh earth free of ice and snow, warmed by the climbing sun, the colorful crocuses. It wasn't spring to Jack. It was just a season of the year when you couldn't play ice hockey.

This Saturday Mason had said he was going to call. He hadn't called. What a day for a drive in the country, for tennis or just a game of catch, for anything except hockey! What a day, what a drab, depressing day!

And then an auto horn blew, an old-fashioned horn, the horn on Mason's car. Jack, puttering around his room on the second floor of the two-family house, jumped to the window, almost out of the window. Mason's battered coupe seemed to have dropped years off its antique chassis. Mason was looking up out of it, grinning. "Come on, Jack. Let's go. And put on a coat and tie; we're gonna stay out for dinner. O.K.?"

Leaning dangerously out of the window, Jack cried, "Sure, swell!" And before ducking in he added, "Swell day, isn't it?"

"You bet," said Mason enthusiastically.

Jack dashed out of the house. His spirits had risen so suddenly that for a few minutes, as they drove through the business district of Mellton, he chose not to speak for fear of breaking the happy spell that had come along with the unexpectedness of a spring zephyr. Then when they got out of the city traffic into the less crowded parkway and were rolling along at a good clip, Jack said, "What's up?"

Jerry took his eyes off the traffic for a few seconds, glanced at Jack, and said, "Wait till you hear."

"What?"

Jerry took his time, driving along with his hands resting lightly on the wheel, his left elbow on the car door. "There's a fellow by the name of Raymond Young, a graduate of M.I.T. He's a cousin of mine. Know what he did?"

"What?"

"He's one of those guys who worked on the atom bomb at Oak Ridge."

"He did?"

"Yes. He's back in Boston now for some more work at M.I.T. And he rang up this morning. He knows I'm going to M.I.T., so he sort of takes an interest, see?"

"Sure."

Mason guided his coupe around a car slowing down for a turn, straightened it out, and continued. "He called up and asked me if I'd like to drive into Boston and see

him. Said he'd treat me to dinner in Chinatown. He's nuts about Chinese food—so am I."

"Me too," said Jack.

"That's fine, because that's what you're gonna eat tonight. You and Ray and I. I told him I usually went out with you on Saturday night, and I said you were going to M.I.T., too. You are, aren't you?" Jerry glanced at Jack.

"Well, uh, well, I'd thought about it."

Jerry grinned. "It doesn't make any difference. After you talk to Ray Young, you'll go to M.I.T. or my name is Boney Ward."

Jack laughed. "Speaking of Boney Ward, there's the pond."

Jerry looked at the pine trees, the sloping hills, the crocuses, and the glistening water where the ice had been. He grinned. "Scene of our triumphs."

"One anyway," said Jack, smiling. "I'll never forget that Cooper game and those borrowed skates."

Jerry's grin turned into a laugh. "That was really something. The marines to the rescue—that is, Manager Maloney. What an ending!"

"By the way," said Jack, "I saw Maloney the other day at Doc's Place, and did he give me the brush-off! What a guy!"

"Yeah," agreed Jerry. "A fair weather friend if ever there was one."

"And I notice we don't get invited to Dick Whittemore's any more, either."

Jerry shrugged his shoulders. "Oh, well, that's the way it goes, I guess. A hero one day, a bum the next—as long

as your fame is built on something like ice. And one look
at the pond today tells you what happens to ice."

Jack was silent. Jerry was right, he thought, absolutely
right. His fame had been based on something as insecure
as ice and one day it just melted away. And next year it
would be the same and the next year. And the year after
that—the big build-up, the big let-down.

"Now when you get out of M.I.T.," Jerry was saying,
"you've got some knowledge in your bean that doesn't fade
away just because the weather changes. You've got something that you can put to use for years and years. Or have
I said all this before?"

"Not in the same words," said Jack, laughing.

Jerry grinned. "No, the words are different. My spiel
is getting smoother. But don't listen to me; just wait and
listen to Ray Young."

THEY WERE IN BOSTON'S CHINATOWN:
lanterns, curious Chinese letters, a smell of incense, chop-
sticks, teacups without handles, Chinese waiters with
quick, quiet movements. Their waiter was a young man
with a soft voice, a friendly grin, and a smooth glide that
carried him quickly from the kitchen to their table. He
brought them steaming exotic dishes—bright green pep-
pers, tender bamboo shoots, crisp fried noodles and al-
monds, little squares of pork, and dark, salty soy sauce.
Under Ray Young's direction they mixed their dishes according to the local custom, so that each plate was
crammed with a third of each large order, spooned on
top of a bed of fluffy white rice and freely sprinkle with
soy sauce. Jack found the food so delicious that he was
halfway through his first plate before he took a good look
at Ray Young.

At first glance, Ray Young was not very impressive. He
was short and rather thin. He was, Jack figured, somewhere between twenty-five and thirty. Physically he was

not impressive like, for example, Dick Whittemore or Johnny Nolan; but in his face were lively humor and mental agility. The face was alert, and the mind behind it was interesting and interested. At the moment, Ray Young was interested in China.

"I want to go out there in a year or so," said Ray Young. "Must be a wonderful place. Fellows I know, classmates at M.I.T., have gone out there and they're crazy about the country. Shanghai, Tientsin, Chung-king. And they like American engineers out there"—Ray grinned—"especially M.I.T. men. But, seriously, it must be a wonderful country. It gets a hold on Americans in spite of all the poverty and squalor they find there."

Jack and Jerry were listening closely. They were both thinking how wonderful it would be to get on a ship or a plane and go to China as American engineers.

"Every day," said Ray Young, "I thank my lucky stars I had the good sense to go to M.I.T. All over the world an M.I.T. degree is a sort of magic passport. As a matter of fact, I had very little to do with the decision that sent me to M.I.T. In fact there were times when I rebelled against going. But my father knocked enough sense into my head to make me go." Ray Young took a big mouthful of chow mein, chewed and sighed. "Boy, this is good." He chewed for a minute or two and then continued. "He bullied me into going to M.I.T., and that's how I happened to be working at Oak Ridge."

The boys stopped eating and leaned forward. Ray looked at them over his glasses. "You want to know something about atomic energy?"

"You bet we do," said Jerry.

"O.K., wait till I finish this mouthful." They waited. Ray finished. "Well, don't get the idea that we know much about atomic energy. We're still at the very beginning. But every day I spent at Oak Ridge I thanked heaven that my father had had the sense to send me to M.I.T., to make me become one of the people who helped bring all this about."

Ray lifted his small round teacup and drank some of the hot rose-colored tea.

"What was Oak Ridge like?" asked Jack.

"Terrific," said Ray. "We had a five hundred mile plant for the separation of uranium. Seventy buildings on six hundred acres. You see, we had to convert uranium, a solid, into a gas, and mix it with something else. What we got as a result was some stuff that was deadly poisonous and could eat into things nitric acid couldn't even nibble. What stuff! Our chemists sweated to find coatings that would hold it.

"The incidental information we turned up at Oak Ridge," said Ray, "was almost as interesting as the main show. Someone figured that we, that is, the people on the project, discovered five thousand products and processes, just things that popped up as we went from one obstacle to another.

"But the big thing is this, and don't forget it—atomic energy is in its infancy. We're just beginning, and you two can get in it right at the very beginning. We've made the first big step; we've broken up uranium 235 and released a terrific amount of energy in doing it. In addition we know this: we know we can smash an atom of U 235 with a neutron and get an atom of barium and an atom

of krypton. Do you know how many electric volts are released when that split takes place? Two hundred million!" Ray let that sink in before he went on. "This split-up releases several neutrons so that we have a self-sustaining supply of them. And we can control these atomic chain reactions. This much we have discovered. The key has been turned in the lock, the door is open, and here we are—the three of us—standing on the threshold. That's why I say this—anyone who has a chance to go to M.I.T. now, as the atomic era opens, anyone who has a feeling for science and who doesn't take that chance, ought to have his head examined."

SUMMER FOLLOWED SPRING. SCHOOLS closed, heat drifted in over Boston and all its suburbs, including Mellton. The steaming streets were filled with dirty, red-faced kids trying to cool off but succeeding only in getting hotter, squirting hoses on each other, wrestling in the torrents that came tumbling forth from open fire hydrants, eating ice-cream cones till their nickels gave out.

Jerry's car, which had seen a lot of service in the cold months of winter, now became as useful as an ambulance in an emergency. For with it Jerry and Jack could get away from the teeming streets of Mellton. One sweltering day as they drove toward a beach on the Massachusetts shore south of Boston, Jerry said, "We're certainly lucky; I'd hate to be stuck back there in Mellton on a day like this."

"I would be if you hadn't come along," said Jack.

"I didn't mean it that way," said Jerry, grinning. "I'm not the Animal Rescue League."

Jack laughed. "Maybe you're just from the dog pound.

Anyway what a difference it makes, eh? Four wheels and a gasoline engine make all the difference in the world. Fifty years ago in a big city on a summer day we would have been stuck. But just because some engineers . . ."

"You see? There it is again, Jack—engineering."

"Sure, engineering. And fifty years from today we'll get in our atomic planes and be at the beach in a matter of minutes."

"Let's hope so, anyway."

"But after all, Jerry, this engine is practically atomic. Listen to it. Hear those neutrons colliding?"

"Lay off this engine," said Jerry, "or you'll walk to the beach."

Near the beach was an amusement park, a roller coaster. They paid their fares eagerly and jumped into the last seat in the last car. They were cool now, refreshed from a swim in the cold salt water. Their bodies seemed to have shrunk from the contact with the ocean and felt hard and healthy against their clothes.

The little cars clattered around the curve and climbed out of a network of wooden timbers. Now they were moving slowly up a long incline, and below them was the amusement park, the beach, blue water, white surf. Now they were at the summit. For a few brief seconds they saw everything from the highest point in the amusement park—people, automobiles, beach, ocean, all far below. Then they gasped for breath as they were suddenly catapulted into space, hurled down an incline so steep that it seemed like one sheer breath-taking drop. Eyes staring, mouths open, they clung to the guard rail. Up and down again, not so steep or so fast this time. They flew around

THEY GASPED FOR BREATH AS THEY CATAPULTED INTO SPACE.

corners, climbed more hills, dipped sharply, gasped and laughed, and finally clattered around a corner and came to a stop—end of the ride.

Cool, hungry, tired, they ate hot dogs with streaks of yellow mustard and drank big glasses of orangeade. Never, they thought, had they tasted anything so delicious.

They drove back from the beach as the sun set, and Jerry took a different road from the one that had led them to the shore.

"Where we going?" said Jack.

"Over by the Charles River. There's an outdoor concert on the Esplanade."

"Oh. I'm not much on music."

"Neither am I. But I like to hear it outdoors. And besides it's free."

"It better be," said Jack. "I have about two bits left."

The music came from an orchestra seated in a shell-shaped enclosure. The music floated up and out of the shell and into the night air, the sound of violins and oboes and horns.

"Have you noticed that group of buildings across the river?"

"Sure," said Jack. "Do you think I don't know where M.I.T. is? Listen, Jerry. I'm just as anxious to get over there as you are. Like your cousin, Ray Young, said, atomic energy is just getting started. We'll be in on it right at the start. Think of what that can mean. And when the going gets tough, we ought to think of what we'll miss if we start slipping."

"Right."

JERRY'S CAR MADE ALL THE DIFFERENCE IN the world that sweltering summer. Old as it was, it took them to places where salt breezes blew and the sun was a welcome friend instead of an enemy to be dodged all day long. But the car needed help in its old age. And in repairing it they learned a good deal about internal combustion engines, pistons, spark plugs, points, rings, king pins.

One summer day, at Jack's suggestion, they started out for the East Boston airport to see the new big planes that fly regularly from the United States across the Atlantic. But Jerry's old engine, which had been throbbing with a healthy beat, suddenly began to cough, and although Jerry pumped frantically on the accelerator, the engine gasped, choked, and died. Horns honked behind them.

They jumped out, pushed the coupe to one side of the street, opened the hood, and peered in. Jerry shook his head. "Looks like the carburetor."

"Let's get a push back to your house and go to work on it," said Jack.

"O.K."

Finally they reached home after a jolting and nerve-racking ride in front of a delivery wagon's bumper. Taking the carburetor apart, they found it clogged with bits of sediment, little pieces of rubber.

"I thought so," said Jerry. "Once we clean it, we're all set."

"I dunno about that," said Jack.

"Whad'ya mean?"

Jack rubbed his face on his sleeve, wiped his black and greasy hands on a rag. "Well, where is that stuff coming from, that stuff that's spitting up into the carburetor?"

Jerry was silent for a minute, frowning. "You mean you think it's . . ."

"Yeah," said Jack, "I do. I think all that stuff is being pumped up from a dirty tank. If it's the tank, Jerry, you and I aren't going to see any planes flying into the airport today."

It was the tank. And the job of cleaning it took them till sundown. But it was worth it, they thought, to hear the old engine running smoothly again. And they had been so absorbed in their work that they had forgotten the heat. When they finished and drove the car around the block on a trial run, they felt a deep feeling of satisfaction over the successful completion of a job that had at first looked like a very unpleasant and irksome one.

IT WAS AT THE AIRPORT THE NEXT DAY
that they heard the engineer, a man with a sun helmet
and a shirt open on a sunburned neck, say something
that stuck in their minds. The engineer was supervising
the construction of a new runway at one end of the field
and the boys boldly approached him, waited until he had
a few minutes to spare, and started asking questions. He
told them about the length and strength of runways,
asked some questions himself, and smiled a little at their
youthful enthusiasm about anything concerned with engineering. He waved a sunburned, freckled hand through
the hot summer air. "Look around you and see how that
applies to this airport. Those planes coming in." They
looked. "See that one?" said the engineer. They stared at

a growing speck in the sky. The speck grew larger and they could make out its shape, its four engines, its sloping, silver nose, its three-fin tail, its tricycle landing gear. "Constellation," said the engineer, face tilted toward the incoming plane. "Cruises at about three hundred miles an hour. Carries about fifty people from here to England."

They stared.

"What kind of engines does it have?" said Jack.

The engineer smiled. "Now don't ask me too much about aeronautics. That's an entirely different field. But I happen to know that plane. She has Wright Cyclone engines, twenty-two thousand horsepower apiece. And they use about three hundred and fifty gallons of gas an hour. I know its landing weight too, because I build the runways that she drops on. Her landing weight is about seventy-five thousand pounds. But I'm no aeronautical engineer. Engineering covers a lot of ground these days. There are civil engineers like me, electrical engineers, aeronautical engineers, all kinds. Sooner or later you fellows'll have to decide which field of engineering you're going into. Maybe it'll be aviation. By the time you become engineers, they'll be flying six-engine planes carrying a couple of hundred passengers. You'll be working on an atomic engine that'll make jet propulsion old-fashioned. Who knows?" The engineer shook his head. "I don't. But I do know this. You boys'll never have a dull moment in engineering. And whatever part of the world you work in, you'll be useful citizens, doing what my old professor used to repeat over and over again, 'directing the great sources of power in nature for the use and convenience of man.'"

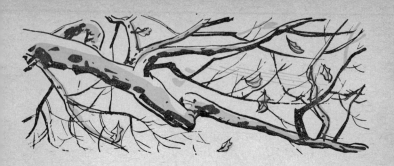

THE HEAT SPELLS BECAME SHORTER. THE
air became cooler. The sun set earlier. The leaves withered
and fell. Then came a real frost. Magically and myster-
iously, an insignificant puddle on Harley Street near
Jack's house was given a pretty pane of glass, which when
stepped on by the inevitable foot of the inevitable boy
shattered into a thousand pieces—slivers, oblongs, rec-
tangles of ice.

Jack noticed the puddle as he came out of his house one
December morning to greet Jerry Mason who had developed the habit of driving Jack to school when the old
battered coupe was willing and able. At the sight of the
ice in the street, almost as many thoughts occurred to
Jack as there were pieces of broken ice. And they were
all associated with ice hockey. First of all, he thought, the
hockey season is almost here and I'm captain of the Trent
hockey team. That thought repeated itself several times.
It was like pumping air into a bicycle tire. At each stroke
of the pump the importance of the title and position
swelled. Captain of the Trent team, captain of the championship Trent hockey team, and said by experts to be a
worthy successor to the immortal Johnny Nolan.

Jerry drove up, honking the horn. "Hi, Jack!"

"Hi, Jerry! Look, ice!"

"Yeah, I know. There's a thin sheet of it on the pond."

"There is?"

"Yeah. Pretty thin, though. Wouldn't hold Captain Jack Taylor and his championship Trent team."

Jack's face reddened a little as Jerry's words matched his thoughts. Jumping into the car, he laughed and said: "I know. But Plaxon's will freeze if we get another day of this. Then we can start practice. I'll go down and talk to Boney at lunchtime."

"He'll prob'ly buttonhole you as soon as we get inside the door this morning," said Jerry, sending the coupe forward. "You know old Boney and how he worried about winning the championship."

"Well, so did we."

"Yeah, but it means more to Boney."

"How come?"

"Oh, cut it out, Jack." Jerry's tone was derisive.

"Whad'ya mean?" Jack's surprise seemed genuine.

"I mean money. There's money in hockey—you know that."

"In high school hockey?" It was Jack's turn to be derisive.

"Well, maybe not in high school hockey, although we made money in that Garden game with City High. But there's money in semi-pro hockey and plenty of money in pro hockey. And I happen to know that Boney's got an interest in a semi-pro team."

"So what?"

"Well, figure it out. It certainly doesn't hurt Boney to

have his team win the metropolitan championship twice in a row, does it, to get his pan in the papers? All that publicity is free advertising. It doesn't do Boney any harm at all."

"No," said Jack slowly, "I guess it doesn't. Still there's nothing wrong with that."

"I didn't say there was. I just said there are reasons why Boney will come chasing you instead of your chasing Boney, and one of the reasons is that you're captain and star of the Trent team."

"Thanks," said Jack.

"You're welcome," said Jerry, grinning. "Trent has the championship team, and you're the star Boney made."

"He did like heck," said Jack indignantly.

"Oh, yes, he did. The papers said so and in a small way it's true. We've learned some hockey from Boney."

"I learned my hockey in pick-up games on the big pond and on little ponds all over the place," said Jack. "I did learn something from Boney; he taught me something about shooting, but most of it was already there and Boney knows it as well as I do."

"Maybe he knows it," said Jerry, "but he's not telling it. Oh, well, Boney's all right in his way."

"Sure, he's not really a bad guy," said Jack. "I remember that Cooper game. Boney didn't get sore when I messed up that skate deal; he just took over and straightened it out."

"That's right," said Jerry. "Of course he didn't exactly want to lose that game. It had something to do with winning the championship."

"O.K. O.K." said Jack.

J ERRY, IT PROVED, WAS RIGHT. BONEY
Ward was on tap, appearing suddenly out of nowhere in
the noisy, crowded high school corridor. His voice was
as smooth as honey. "Oh, Jack . . ."

"Oh, hello, Coach."

Boney smiled the old toothy smile and put his hand on
Jack's shoulder, the same old hand that could be a claw
or a hand depending on the coach's mood. "Hello, Jerry.
How are ya, boy?"

"O.K., Coach."

"Well, Jack, looks like the time has come to defend our hard-won championship. There's ice on the pond. If the temperature stays down where it should, we'll have practice tomorrow. Plaxon's rink. I've got it all sewed up. We're gonna be the first on that ice, by golly. Nothing too good for a championship team, y'know."

"That's swell, Coach."

"And I've got some new hockey sticks, top grade hickory; just got 'em in from Canada. Take more than the Thatcher brothers to break those sticks." The coach grinned. "You remember those Thatcher brothers, don't you, Jack—in the Cooper game? Remember the skates you left behind?" Boney smiled. "And we got 'em out just in the nick of time, didn't we, Jack boy?"

"Sure, I remember how you came to the rescue that day, Coach," said Jack.

"Oh, well." Boney gave his thin lips a twist and assumed a modest pose. "After all, boys, that's what a coach is for. You're the fellas who do the work and take the chances out there on the ice. I'm just there to guide and direct and help out the best I can." Boney's voice changed suddenly to an obsequious tone. "Oh, good morning, Mr. Findley."

It was the Principal.

"Good morning, Boney. 'Morning, Taylor. 'Morning, Mason. Planning another championship?"

"Hope so, Mr. Findley," said Boney modestly.

"Well, you certainly did a bang-up job last year, Boney, and you too, boys. Good luck, and stay eligible."

Mr. Findley smiled and passed on down the corridor, nodding to left and right like a king entering his palace.

"You heard that, boys," said Boney huskily. "Shows what Mr. Findley thinks of our team. Everybody's watching us this year, fellas; you know, they always watch a champ. And for heaven's sake, fellas, remember what Mr. Findley said and stay eligible."

With these words of warning Coach Boney Ward strode off down the corridor with a few nods to favored seniors.

"Know what?" said Jerry.

"What?"

"His name shouldn't be Boney Ward; it should be Baloney Ward."

"Aw, lay off Boney. He's not so bad," said Jack. "And say things like that softly. Boy! If that ever got back to Boney—whew! You'd be ineligible all right, and it wouldn't be for failing math, either."

"That kind of ineligibility wouldn't bother me," said Mason earnestly. "But it certainly would bother me if I started flunking trig or solid geometry."

"Me too," said Jack.

THE COLD SPELL MADE ICE ON PLAXON'S rink, as Jack and Boney Ward had prophesied. Jack skated out on it with all the old sensations of power and speed, plus pleasant new ones that stemmed from being captain of the Trent team.

Once more he experienced the wonderful feeling of tight, sharp skates skimming over hard ice, biting into it, sailing swiftly over it, creating a cold wind that blew gently against the skater's face and whistled in his eardrums. There was satisfaction too in his uniform—the red-white-and-blue jersey, the padded pants, the long, dark blue stockings, and the padded leather gauntlets. Jack found pleasure in the way his teammates addressed him, in their respect and admiration, and in the awe of the hangers-on at Plaxon's rink, young and old. Then there was the press—the school paper, first of all, with a fine glossy picture of Jack in his uniform, crouching and grinning; and more important still, pictures in the city papers of Captain Jack Taylor, leader of the champion-

ship Trent team. Sometimes there were even statements. "Jack Taylor predicts second championship in a row for Trent. 'I think we have the stuff,' said the Trent star when interviewed yesterday by a *Tribune* reporter." But most of the statements were handed out by Boney Ward, whose homely face and toothy smile were appearing in the press with surprising frequency.

Early in his junior year, Jack had looked upon hockey practice with apprehension. So much had depended on his showing at each session, particularly in the first of the season. Now all the nervousness and tension had vanished. Now practice at Plaxon's was just another proof of his skill and importance. Lured by the publicity following the capture of the league championship, a score of candidates turned out for the Trent hockey team, all anxious to climb aboard the winning band-wagon, to be the pupils and associates of the famous Coach Boney Ward, and teammates of the dazzling star, Jack Taylor.

The big squad had to be cut and Ward had many conferences with Jack about the candidates.

"Now you'll get some idea of the headaches of being a coach, Jack," said Boney, this clear cold afternoon at Plaxon's rink. His friendly hand, never a claw these days, was resting affectionately on Jack's shoulder. There was no rasp in his friendly voice except when from time to time it was called upon to straighten out a tangle on the ice.

"Now our first line is, of course, O.K.," said Boney complacently. "And we've got Jerry Mason on defense. But," and Boney's voice began to rasp, "we stop right there. Those birds who go around saying, 'No wonder

.... THE WONDERFUL FEELING OF SKIMMING OVER HARD ICE.

Boney wins championships; he's got the material,' are just so many bull-throwers, Jack. And that reminds me. That little interview you gave out to the *Tribune*." Jack's face reddened. But Boney's voice was friendly, fatherly. "Send those reporters to me, Jack. I'll handle 'em. They have a way of getting people to say things they don't mean, see?"

"O.K., Coach," Jack mumbled.

"Mind you, I'm not criticizing," said Boney. "But just look at our material. Just take a look out there on the ice. Whad'ya see? A tangle of arms, legs, and skates. Do you see a championship team out there? Of course not. But a lot of guys go around saying Boney this and Boney that and how could he miss with all that material. It makes me sick to hear that tripe. Some day I'm gonna nail one of those birds and get him out here and make him eat his words or, better still, take a poke at him.

"Well"—Boney let the rasp die out of his voice—"it all comes with fame, Jack. You and I are riding high now, and all the jealous bums are bound to take potshots at us."

Jack nodded. He didn't exactly know who the jealous bums were, but he assumed that they moved in coaching circles and hung around places like the Garden. Anyway, he thought, it was interesting and exciting. Boney wasn't a bad egg, a little corny perhaps, but he certainly seemed to know what the score was.

"So far," said Boney, "we got four players on our team. And the first game is just a week away. That'll give you an idea of what a coach is faced with, Jack. Oh, well," Boney sighed, "let's get on with it. Lessee, two goalies—

McGuire and Jones. I think McGuire's got the edge, don't you, Jack?"

"Definitely," said Jack. McGuire moved smoothly and compactly in the cage; Jones was slower and left openings.

"I hate to drop a kid like Jones; it'll hurt him. And I hate to hurt kids; but they've gotta start takin' the knocks sooner or later, don't they, Jack?"

"I guess so," said Jack. He was thinking back to how he had felt when in sophomore year his name had been missing on the list posted on the bulletin board. Yes, he thought, it would be a tough knock for Jones. But, as Boney said, you had to start taking the knocks sooner or later. Boney wasn't a bad guy at heart.

"Now on defense," said Boney, "we got Mason, of course, and Shilepsky and this Thompson kid. Thompson's good, but Shilepsky is bigger and tougher, and we need someone big and tough to dish out the body checks."

"Thompson's learning fast, though," said Jack. "And he's quick on his skates."

"Yeah, that's right, Jack." Boney rubbed his chin. O.K., we'll keep 'em both. Shilepsky's first string, Thompson as sub. We need a good sub on defense. Last year we were just lucky. Oh, well, you need luck in this game. O.K. First line as it stands, of course, Second line . . . . What about this Newton boy?"

Jack looked out on the rink and saw a redheaded sixteen-year-old lead a line down the ice, skating fast and dribbling deftly. "Not bad," said Jack. "I'd say Newton is about the best of the bunch."

"And those kids with him aren't so bad either—Barnes

and Mario. They look better than those other lines out there." Boney wagged his head. "How these kids expect to play hockey without knowing how to skate—holy mackerel!"

Jack grinned. He could remember when he had learned to skate; it seemed like a long, long time ago.

"Well," said Boney, "I think we've got it—goalie, defense, forwards. O.K., and it's about time. Only a week to the Hurlbutt game."

After practice Jack and Jerry drove to Doc's Place. Jack hadn't seen much of Jerry at practice; Boney Ward had taken up most of his time. In fact, Jack reflected, he had seen increasingly less of Jerry in the last couple of weeks. There had been so many new duties connected with the captaincy. Meetings with Boney, meetings with the new manager, and of course meetings with the press. Jack was glad to have a few minutes alone with Jerry now to tell him about the new team: McGuire, the goalie, and how well he handled himself in the cage; Shilepsky and Thompson, the new defensemen. "You agree on that, don't you, Jerry? After all, your opinion is pretty valuable. You're a veteran defenseman."

"They're O.K.," said Jerry.

"Then we've got an entirely new line by the redhead, Newton. How's it look?"

"Not bad," said Jerry.

"I think we've got the makings," said Jack. "Boney and I talked it over this afternoon. The list goes up tomorrow. Gosh, remember when we used to wait for that list and how we felt when our names weren't on it? Gee, I re-

member in sophomore year when my name didn't make it. I felt rotten. Oh, well, things have changed."

"They certainly have," said Jerry. "Say, there was something I wanted to talk to you about. Oh, never mind." They had reached Doc's Place. "We can talk about it inside."

"Sure," said Jack.

But there was no time to talk about it inside, because as soon as Jack came in the calls of welcome and the slaps on the back began, and Jerry found himself edged to one side by the admirers and the hangers-on. Jack held court at the center table, while the girls sitting at the soda fountain watched enviously, talked idly, twisted around, and did their best to attract the attention of the captain, the hockey star. He was not as good-looking as Dick Whittemore, but he was certainly presentable enough, with his neatly combed black hair, his slight build, his easy graceful movements; and, they told themselves, he was much better dressed than last year.

Fifteen minutes of noise, confusion, and adulation were enough for Jerry. Catching Jack's eye with an effort, he said, "I've got to shove, Jack. You coming or are you gonna stay?"

Surprised, Jack looked up from his circle of admirers. "Oh, wait a minute, Jerry."

"I can't. I've got a lotta work to do on solid geometry."

"Gee, I oughta get in some work, too," said Jack, turning down the corners of his mouth. "Say, Jerry, you wanted to talk to me about something."

"Some other time," said Jerry.

"O.K. So long!"

"So long!"

As Jerry walked out, Jack thought, Something's wrong; something's off the track.

But just then McGuire, the new goalie, came in. Jack called to him. "Hey, McGuire! Come on over. I've got some news for you." And as McGuire came over, his face red and expectant, Jack held out his hand and said, "How does it feel to be goalie of the championship Trent team?"

McGuire's mouth opened, his eyes widened. "You mean I made it?" he said.

"I mean you're in, kid," said Jack. "Have a drink on me, any five-cent drink."

The crowd laughed. Jack Taylor, they thought, was a worthy successor to Dick Whittemore as far as personality was concerned and, what's more, a far better hockey player.

JACK FOUND OUT WHAT JERRY WANTED TO talk about the next night when Boney Ward called up. Boney's voice was harsh. "That pal of yours has turned in his uniform!"

"Who?" said Jack, knowing but unable to believe it.

"Your friend, Jerry Mason. How do you like that? Here we are, all set to put that championship in the bag second year in a row, and he quits, quits cold."

"But gee, Coach! Holy smoke! I don't believe it. He wasn't ineligible."

" 'Course he wasn't," snapped Boney. "Not even close. But he said he was worried about solid geometry—the dirty rat."

Jack flared up. "Now listen, Boney. Jerry's a good friend of mine and . . ."

"He is, is he? You listen to me, young man. He quit cold, didn't he? He walked out on us."

"Maybe he did. But if he did, he had good reason to.

My marks aren't so hot either, if I expect to make M.I.T. next fall."

"Now listen, Jack," said Boney, and oil spilled forth on the troubled waters. "I didn't mean anything personal. It was just that this struck me all of a sudden. You know how much work I've, er, you and I have put into that team. I think we can win the championship again, boy. And then this hits me out of the blue. Now I have nothing against Jerry personally. I always thought he was a nice kid; you know, the quiet studious type. But gee, Jack, quitting just before the opening game of the season! If he'd only given me a little notice, a couple of weeks, say, time enough to break Thompson in. If he'd just play in a couple of games. But no! he just walks out cold, and that kinda stuff don't go with me, Jack. I was sore, but you can see how I feel."

"Sure, Boney, you're right. He should have given us a couple weeks' notice, played in a game or two, anyway. Suppose I ring him up and try to talk him into it."

"No, I wouldn't do that if I were you." Boney gave a little laugh. "Ya see, we had quite a run-in, him and me. We had quite an argument. I was pretty sore, I guess, and I used some pretty strong words. I doubt very much if Mason would, er, reconsider. No, we'll just have to break Thompson in. Well, just wanted to let you know, Jack old boy. See you at practice tomorrow."

"O.K., Coach." Jack hung up. Too bad. Jerry was a nice guy. That solid geometry was no snap, either. He'd have to bone up on it himself—but not during hockey season.

When Jack met Jerry at school the next day, Jerry said, "I suppose you heard about the row I had with Boney?"

"Yeah. I wish you coulda let us know a little sooner."

"Listen, Jack"—Jerry's voice was thin and metallic—"I told you over and over again, off the ice and on it, summer and winter, that beside M.I.T. hockey didn't mean a damn to me and if anything interfered with my going to M.I.T. that thing, whatever it was, was going to be eliminated."

Jack lashed back. "Even if it means eliminating your friends?"

Jerry was angry now. "You can take it that way if you like. If you think for one minute that I'm going to let you and Boney Ward and a hockey team keep me from getting into M.I.T., you're wacky!"

"Oh, yeah? Leaving people in the lurch doesn't seem to bother you. It doesn't matter to you that we've worked two years to build up a championship team. You'd just as soon walk out and wreck it."

Jerry took in a deep breath, snorted it out, and snapped back. "Put it any way you like! Hash it over with Boney Ward. Hand it out to the papers! Do anything you like. *But I'm through with hockey.* Don't forget that."

"I won't forget it," said Jack bitterly.

BONEY WARD WAS SPEAKING, ONE FOOT on the locker room bench, his hands in his pockets. Sitting in two rows in clean uniforms, their tightly laced skates safely placed on the boardwalk that ran between the benches, the members of the Trent hockey team raised their faces in respectful attention. Boney started softly: "Well, here we are, where we were just a year ago, some of us, coming up for the first game. And I said then, you veterans will remember"—Boney smiled silkily at his star and let the benevolent smile slide on to Newman and Schwartz—"I said then you always have to win the first one. And I was right." Boney shifted his position, took one hand out of his pocket, rested his elbow on his thigh, and leaned forward. "Well, here we are starting out all over again down the long road that may lead to another championship. It seems like a long road, but you'd be surprised how quick you go over it. At each crossing you find another team waiting, trying to knock you off the road, see? Now all we're gonna think about

today is the team at the first crossing, Hurlbutt High. Now, from what I hear, they got a fair team, not too good, not too bad. One first-class player, Sanders, their center. Watch him. And remember the things you've learned in practice. Newton, keep your line together. Thompson, stay close to Shilepsky. Play together as a team! And just think of one thing—beat Hurlbutt!"

"Good old Boney," Jack thought with a grin, as he clumped out at the head of the file of Trent players.

"Here they come," cried a spectator and the big Trent gallery let out a cheer.

"Quite a crowd, quite a crowd," said Boney, smiling his toothy smile. "Listen to that, Jack."

"Yea Yea Yea, rah, rah, rah, Taylor! Taylor! Taylor!" yelled the Trent supporters.

Jack felt his flesh tingle.

"There's nothing like a championship team," said Boney. "Nothing like it. O.K., Jack, go out there and make a monkey out of that Sanders."

Jack grinned and said, "O.K., Boney." He motioned to his team. "Let's go, fellas." He skated gracefully out on the slick ice of Plaxon's rink and the crowd broke into applause. The applause rose up all around the rink from supporters of Hurlbutt, supporters of Trent, and neutral spectators. For this was the championship team with the best player in the league, Jack Taylor, and as they skated out onto the ice in their bright uniforms they looked like champions.

A few minutes later Jack was shaking hands with the Hurlbutt captain, while a photographer took a picture. Then nonchalantly he drew on his leather gauntlets

JACK BACKHANDED THE PUCK INTO THE NETS. GOAL!

again and skated toward the referee for the face-off. The whistle blew and the expectant crowd let out a yell.

The yell grew into a roar as Jack trapped the puck on his stick, circled with flashing skates, and opened up with all the speed and power that made him the best player in the league. It was something to see, that speed that came out of those skates as they bit in hard at first, with a sharp one-two, one-two cadence, then almost flew as top speed and momentum were attained and all the body needed was an expert flick of either skate for added power and guidance.

The roar of the crowd grew as Jack flashed by Sanders, the Hurlbutt center, leaving him floundering, his skates stumbling, his stick flailing the air. The two Hurlbutt defensemen wiggled backwards on their skates, their eyes fastened on the figure flying toward them. The Hurlbutt right defenseman thought he saw Jack swerve to the left and took three quick fatal steps on his skates, leaving a small corridor of open ice between himself and his teammate. Then he saw what was going to happen and stopped abruptly, almost knocking himself down in his anxiety, and threw himself back toward his alarmed teammate. But it was too late. As the crowd yelled, Jac swerved in and split the defense!

The Hurlbutt goalie suddenly found himself all alone, unguarded, with the league's best player just a few yards away and coming like a whirlwind. The Hurlbutt goalie dived (although some Trent fans later said he fainted). Jack dribbled the puck around him as he plunged forward and backhanded it into the nets. Goal!

The crowd roared. A Trent fan rang a cowbell, another

blew a horn. The Hurlbutt left defenseman said: "What-sa matter, ya dope? Didn'tcha see what he was gonna do?" And the Hurlbutt right defense snarled back: "No, I didn't. And you didn't either, ya goop."

A few minutes later, in the lull that came after Jack scored his second goal, a tall well-dressed figure wearing an expensive blue overcoat appeared at Boney Ward's side and intoned smoothly, "Well, Boney, looks as if you've got another championship."

Boney turned and recognized Shaftesbury Sedgwick. He rose at once. "Hello, Mr. Sedgwick. So you came to give our team the once-over! Well, how does it look?"

"It looks excellent, Boney," said Mr. Sedgwick in his rich voice. "And in some places"—Mr. Sedgwick gave Boney a knowing smile—"in some places, Boney, and I think you know what I mean, it looks even better than that."

Boney grinned. "Yeah, I think I know what you mean, Mr. Sedgwick. Well, it's been some time since Trent has had a real star like Johnny Nolan. By the way, Mr. Sedgwick, how is Johnny Nolan? I hear he got out of the Army."

Mr. Sedgwick avoided Boney's searching eyes. "Yes, that's right, Boney. He's out."

"Is he back with your firm, Mr. Sedgwick?" Boney pursued.

"Well, no, Boney, he isn't." Mr. Sedgwick stroked his mustache. "He's, uh, getting readjusted. You know how it is, Boney. The boys who went away to war went through a lot and it'll take some time for them to get back to the old routine. Of course we held his old job

open for him," said Mr. Sedgwick. "But he's not the same old Johnny Nolan, Boney. He doesn't seem to have the old get-up-and-go. In fact, I heard he's gone back to college, graduate work, wants to teach or something. Fantastic. Oh, well." Mr. Sedgwick shrugged his expensively covered shoulders. "It's one of those things. But what I wanted to say, Boney, was that I want to talk to this Taylor boy. I'd like him to have dinner with me at the club day after tomorrow."

"Oh, sure, sure, Mr. Sedgwick. I'll tell him. Have ya got to leave? Why don't you stay awhile? Sit right down here beside me and watch the game."

Mr. Sedgwick smiled smoothly. "No, thanks, Boney, old man. I've seen what I wanted to see. I've got to be going. You've done a fine job, Boney, a fine job."

Boney purred, "Thanks, Mr. Sedgwick; thanks a lot. Glad you think so. G'by, Mr. Sedgwick." And to himself he said: But I'm going to talk to the boy first, Mr. Sedgwick. I'm going to talk to him first. You're just a little bit too late, Mr. Sedgwick.

TRENT WON ITS FIRST GAME, 6-2. JACK
Taylor scored four of Trent's goals. "Taylor stars," said
the papers. "Trent sensation opens season with scoring
splurge. 'I wouldn't be surprised if he won the championship again,' said Boney Ward in an interview."

School the next day was a triumphant procession for
Jack. There were admiring cries, slaps on the back. Even
two of the teachers smiled and said, "Well, we have a
celebrity in our midst." But the solid geometry teacher
didn't smile. Jack had an uncomfortable time during that
period. There was a quiz and he knew that he fell down

badly on it. But there wasn't much time to worry about it, for a group of admirers came whooping along between classes and swept Jack away on a tide of popularity.

Jack had entertained vague thoughts about studying math after school, but several hearty invitations and pleas of "Aw, come on, Jack," rather easily persuaded him that a short visit to Doc's Place was in order. It was there that Boney Ward found him. Jack didn't mind leaving at Boney's request. He had enjoyed half an hour of adulation and, besides, it looked important for Boney to come after him and ask him for a few minutes of private conversation. The crowd in Doc's Place was impressed.

"Uh, there was something I wanted to talk to you about," said Boney. "I thought we'd better talk about it right now before the season gets too far advanced."

Jack sat mystified in Boney's car.

Boney continued, "We'll go to a place I know, down near the Garden. O.K. with you?"

"I guess so," said Jack slowly.

"Swell," said Boney. "Matter of fact," he added importantly, "we're prob'ly gonna play two or three games in the Garden this season."

"Oh," said Jack without enthusiasm.

"Whatsa matter?" said Boney. "Don't you like the Garden?"

"Oh, sure," said Jack. "The Garden's all right. It's just that, well, you know, the time we played there it was sort of gloomy—dark, cigar butts, stuff like that."

"Oh, yeah," said Boney, driving the car along the parkway, "I know whatcha mean. But that was a bad day.

You should see the Garden at night for a big college or pro game. You saw it at its worst, Jack, on a Saturday afternoon. It was almost spring then. But to see the Garden on a winter night, why, it's as exciting as Hollywood. And at the pro games when ya get almost twenty thousand people packed in there, think of that, Jack—twenty thousand people!"

"Some crowd," said Jack.

"Sure it is," said Boney. "And they pay some prices, too. But we'll talk about it when we get to the tavern."

As Boney drove through the thickening traffic, Jack thought of the tavern as an inn with a fireplace and a few people sitting in deep leather chairs. He was disappointed at the kind of tavern Boney Ward introduced him to, with its cheap, shabby furniture, its smell of antiseptic and stale cigar smoke, its seedy bartenders and the two drunks with mottled complexions and bloodshot eyes who stood arguing at the bar.

Boney, Jack noticed, seemed to be well known here. The bartenders greeted him out of the corners of their mouths and a man standing at the bar said, "Hi, Boney."

"We'll get a booth," said Boney. "The Ripper should be here any minute now."

Jack, trying not to breathe deeply of the foul air, said, "Who's the Ripper?"

"You mean to say you never heard of Ripper Clapham? Why, he's the famous trainer of the big pro teams, one of the best-known characters in the Garden. Quite a player himself in his day, a defenseman. That's how he got the handle, the Ripper. He usta rip 'em all right.

'Course he got ripped once or twice himself. Yes, sir, if there's anything you wanna know about pro hockey, just ask the Ripper. He's got all the answers. But he'll be along. Meanwhile I wanna drink. Waiter," he called "bring me a straight rye with a beer chaser. What about you, Jack?"

"I'll have a coke," said Jack.

"O.K. And one coke. Attaboy, Jack." Boney winked. "Stay on the wagon during the season anyway."

"I don't drink," said Jack.

"Not even an occasional beer?" said Boney.

"Nope, not even beer," said Jack.

"O.K.," said Boney, "I was only kiddin'." He drew a rumpled pack of cigarettes out of his pocket, pulled one out, struck a match, and lit the cigarette. The drinks arrived—a small glass of brown whiskey, a larger glass of amber beer, and a bottle of Coca-Cola. Boney lifted the little glass, took a gulp, made a face, and quickly took a a long draught of beer. Then he sucked on the cigarette and a long streamer of gray smoke came out of his lungs. Jack, watching, saw that all the motions were smooth and well rehearsed. Boney must have been going through them for years—the cigarette, the little glass of whiskey, the glass of beer. The clean cold air, the clean cold ice, seemed far away in another world.

"Now look, Jack. Here's the story. I'm gonna put my cards on the table. You're gettin' to be quite a hockey player, Jack, building up a reputation, getting your name all over the place. That's good, that's fine. But all this is gettin' a little out of hand."

"How d'ya mean?" said Jack.

Boney smiled again. "Well, look, Jack. Lemme put my cards on the table." Boney gestured with his hands as if spreading his cards on the tavern table, including in the gesture a flank attack on the whiskey and beer which he took with a gulp, a wince, and a sigh. "I'm your friend, see, Jack?"

"Sure," said Jack. "Sure."

"Well, look, here's how it is, see? Uh, you haven't got too much money, have you? I mean your family."

"That's right."

"And you'd like to make a lot of money, wouldn't ya?"

"Well . . . sure," said Jack.

"O.K. Fine." Boney finished the whiskey, drained the beer, and said abruptly, "What I'm suggesting is that you think seriously of playing pro hockey."

"Pro hockey!" Jack's eyes popped.

"Pro hockey," said Boney firmly. "You just let me handle everything, kid. Me and the Ripper. We'll take care of everything. We'll have it all done up nice and legal, contract 'n' everything, and ya father's signature 'n' everything. All open and aboveboard."

"But I'm going to college," said Jack. "That is, I hope to if I pass the exams."

"Sure, sure," said Boney. "Of course you're goin' to college. Why not? Play on the Harvard team for a coupla years. Whad'ya think old Sedgwick is smellin' around for? He wants ya to go to college and play for Harvard. Sure he does, and he'll foot every penny of the bill."

"What!" Jack almost shouted the word.

THE RIPPER FLUNG BEER IN BONEY'S FACE.

"Of course," said Boney, his voice rich with worldly wisdom. "Listen, kid, you weren't born yesterday. That's why I wanted to put you wise, see? The world is gonna be at your feet, kid, and all you gotta do is let ol' Boney take over." Boney stubbed out his cigarette. "Hey, waiter! Fill 'em again, will ya?"

Jack was still dazed when Boney greeted the Ripper, a tub-shaped, middle-aged man with a bulbous nose, cauliflower ears, a pearl gray hat with its brim turned down in front and back, and a tan polo coat.

"Hello, Boney," said the Ripper. "Who's this? Why, I know who it is. It's Jack Taylor. Recognized your pitcher from the papers, kid. Put 'er there. Glad to know ya."

Boney beamed. "I was just tellin' Jack about our contract," said Boney. "The kid didn't know he was in a gold mine till I turned on the light." Boney cackled. Jack managed a weak grin.

"Sure," said the Ripper. You'll clean up as a pro, Kid. The league is cryin' for an American star. All we got now is Canadians."

"A Yankee and a Harvard man besides," said Boney. "Terrific."

"Absolutely." The Ripper encircled a glass with a big paw. "Matter of fact, Boney, I can arrange for Jack to get in some practice with one of our pro teams this season."

"You can!" said Boney, pretending to be incredulous. "Whad'ya know about that, Jack?"

Jack was thinking, I've got to get out of here fast. "Look, Boney," he said in a tone of desperation. "I've gotta get going."

"Oh," said Boney, his face falling. "O.K., kid. Well, the Ripper and I'll talk over the contract. We don't wanna rush you, kid, but . . ."

"Sit down!" It was a snarl and the Ripper was behind it, the Ripper with the bulbous nose and the cauliflower ears.

Surprised, alarmed, Jack sank back into his seat.

"We're gonna get this straightened out right now," growled the Ripper. "I didn't come over here to play games. I came over here to do business."

"But you heard what the kid said, Ripper." Boney's voice was weak.

"Never mind what the kid said," pursued the Ripper, his big hands on the table, his eyes fixed on Jack. "He don't know nothin' and I don't know nothin' right now. But when I get through, we're all gonna know somethin'. Now look, kid, it's about time you learned the facts of life."

"Such as what?" said Jack, trying to make his voice firm but knowing it shook.

"Such as this." The Ripper banged a big fist on the table and shook the glasses. "Boney Ward can hem and haw all he wants, but I'm not made that way. I usta play pro hockey, see, pro hockey; and I'm used to takin' it and dishin' it out, either one or the other. But none o' this maybe and but stuff. Now I don't know"—the Ripper lowered his voice to a well-modulated shout—"whether you know this or not, but a few weeks ago your coach here came to me at the Garden and sold me a piece of you, several hundred dollars' worth."

"What!" Jack blurted the word out and stared at

Boney. Boney seemed to have shrunk. His lips moved but no words came out.

"Now when someone nicks me in the place where I keep my folding money, I wanna know what the score is," said the Ripper.

"I'll tell you what the score is," Jack began.

"Shut up!" Boney had finally managed to regain his voice. "This kid made an agreement with me, Ripper," he said, "a verbal agreement in the presence of witnesses. It's just the same as a contract."

For a matter of seconds Jack sat still, stunned for a moment as he had been during the Garden game when Boney flared up. But just for a few seconds. Then his mind reacted with sudden, consuming anger. "Boney," he said quietly, "that's the biggest lie you've told since I've known you, and I've heard you tell some whoppers."

Jack got up as he spoke, thinking. He'll take a poke at me sure.

But Boney didn't move, though rage played like lightning over his face. It was the Ripper who moved, the Ripper who, sensing that Jack was telling the truth, picked up a half-empty glass of beer and flung it full in Boney's face. Then he jumped to his feet with a jerk that almost upset the table. "The kid's tellin' the truth. Anybody could see that, Boney. So get that dough back to me by next month, if you wanna stay healthy."

Boney said nothing. As Jack left without further words to either man, he looked back and saw Boney still sitting in the booth, wiping the beer off his face with a handkerchief, his eyes staring straight ahead, unseeing.

MR. SEDGWICK'S VOICE WAS AS RICH AS the sauce on the duck Jack was eating. "I never realized that my friend Boney was such a stupid fellow. My goodness me"—Mr. Sedgwick clucked his tongue in deprecation—"I'll have to speak to Boney about this. Of course," said Mr. Sedgwick, delicately breaking a hard roll, "there's nothing to be worried about, that is, as far as we're concerned. You haven't signed a contract, you haven't even seen a contract. But you can bet your bottom dollar that anything that Boney and the Ripper cooked up would be definitely advantageous to those two rogues. If *I* have anything to do with it, you won't sign any contract!" Mr. Sedgwick swept up to a stern finish and then, like a runner relaxing after breaking the tape, softened the sternness with a winning smile.

Jack smiled back across the well-filled table. What a difference, he thought, from Boney's sordid tavern. This was the kind of place he had dreamed about, read about in books, seen in movies. A small silver cup, lined with crisp lettuce, filled with fat shrimps, and set in a con-

tainer of cracked ice, had arrived first. Then soup had
been brought in steaming in a silver tureen, cream of
celery soup, also delicious. Next had come a thick, tender
steak flanked by French fried potatoes. And now a chocolate eclair stuffed with vanilla ice cream. What a dinner!

"Now my advice to you, Jack, is this." Mr. Sedgwick
dabbed at his mustache. "Just play along with Boney this
season. After all, a season doesn't last too long. Don't sign
anything; tell your family not to sign anything. And if
Boney gets persistent, just tell him I told you to refer him
to me. I'll handle him.

Jack thought that Shaftesbury Sedgwick looked as if
he could handle anyone, with his poise and his worldly
ways and, of course, his deep rich voice. He looks good,
thought Jack, but sometimes looks can be very deceiving.

Mr. Sedgwick smiled. "Well, now that we've disposed
of Boney Ward, let's discuss your future. You're a senior
finishing this year?"

"Yes, sir," said Jack. "That is, I hope so."

"Hmm, then you're going to Harvard, of course?"

A little red crept into Jack's face. He felt that if he did
not say yes, he would disappoint and possibly hurt Mr.
Sedgwick. He stammered, "Uh, well, er, I was planning
on M.I.T., Mr. Sedgwick."

"Oh, really?" said Mr. Sedgwick, raising his eyebrows.
"M.I.T. Hmm. Well, I know one or two M.I.T. men; not
bad chaps—engineers, you know. They spend their lives inside turbines or some such machinery. We have too many
engineers, too many mechanics. That's why a young man
like you, Jack, should seriously consider a career in the

idea business. That's my business, Jack. You've undoubt-
edly heard of Sedgwick, Harrod, and Wigglesby?"

"Well . . ." Jack began. He never had heard of Sedgwick, Harrod, and Wigglesby, but Mr. Sedgwick paid no
attention.

"My business, Jack, is essentially an idea business." Mr.
Sedgwick produced a gold cigarette case, took out a cigarette, and lit it with a small gold lighter. "You see, we're
in everything—automobiles, airplanes, even atoms; all
these are the tools in our workroom. Any mechanic, Jack,
any engineer can make a turbine work. But Sedgwick,
Harrod, and Wigglesby find a place for that product in
our economic system. In other words, if it weren't for the
idea men, men who bridge the gap between the producer
and the consumer, the whole economic machine would
grind to a devastating halt."

Shaftesbury Sedgwick paused, inhaled smoke, and blew
it towards a chandelier. Then he looked at Jack.

"A young man like you," said Mr. Sedgwick, "stands
at the crossroads."

Jack saw a picture of himself standing at the crossroads.
It was, he thought, a fateful moment.

"Before you," intoned Shaftesbury Sedgwick, "stretch
two roads. The sign on one reads M.I.T., the other, Harvard. Both roads are splendid roads, but in my carefully
considered opinion Harvard is a super-highway. Let me
point out a few good reasons why I think so.

"In my opinion the purpose of a college is to teach a
young man how to think. If he wants to learn a trade, let
him go to a trade school. Well, Jack, Harvard certainly

fills the bill when it comes to teaching young men how to think. Just take a look around this club; look at all these men, all solid, respectable citizens. Sound, that's the word for it, sound. Over there in the corner, for example, is Hastings W. Abbott, vice president of the . . ."

Many of Mr. Sedgwick's rich words seemed to be floating over Jack's head. They seemed to have a gentle, lulling effect and he realized that he was sleepy. The heavy food, the big dinner, or was it Mr. Sedgwick's voice? He concentrated again on what Mr. Sedgwick was saying.

"All of which leads up to this, Jack. You are an outstanding hockey player. You could become, I think, one of the best players Harvard ever had."

"Well, Mr. Sedgwick," Jack began in a modest tone.

Shaftesbury Sedgwick's voice rolled onward. "I wouldn't say that unless I meant it. A couple more seasons, hard work, strict training, and you'll be just the man we want on the Harvard team. But first of all, you should spend a year at prep school to meet the kind of boys you'll want to associate with at Harvard. Yes, I know what you're thinking—the expense. I'll take care of that. We'll arrange a scholarship. You'll like St. Barnes; they have eight hockey rinks."

"Eight hockey rinks!"

"Eight," smiled Mr. Sedgwick. "Everybody plays hockey at St. Barnes. Hockey at St. Barnes is a major sport. Wonderful school. And you'll meet the boys who, when they get to Harvard, are taken into the right clubs. You'll meet boys at St. Barnes who will be your friends through life and very influential friends, too."

Jack nodded.

"Now I want you to think this over, Jack, give it careful consideration."

"It sounds great, Mr. Sedgwick," said Jack. And he thought, Maybe I mean it. A year at St. Barnes, all expenses paid. Imagine, eight hockey rinks, hockey a major sport! It sounds good.

Mr. Sedgwick placed his napkin on the table, pushed back his chair, and smiled. "Well, Jack, I'm glad I caught you when you were standing at the crossroads. And I can assure you of this: when your college career has ended in a blaze of glory, and you stand at the threshold of life with a Harvard diploma in your hand, Sedgwick, Harrod, and Wigglesby will be ready to welcome you into the firm. We want you to be one of us."

"That's fine, Mr. Sedgwick," said Jack.

As they were leaving, Jack, who was floating on a cloud of chocolate eclairs and exclusive clubs, suddenly seemed to look over the edge of the cloud and see the earth below. "Mr. Sedgwick," he said, "whatever became of Johnny Nolan? I heard he was in the Army . . ."

A shadow crossed Mr. Sedgwick's serene face. "Ah, yes, Johnny Nolan. Wonderful hockey player and captain of the Harvard team. He worked for my firm before going into the Army. But the war"—Mr. Sedgwick sadly shook his head now crowned by an expensive hat—"the war has claimed its casualties and I'm afraid Johnny Nolan was one of them."

Jack's voice was surprised. "But I heard he got out all right."

"Oh, yes," said Mr. Sedgwick, "he's out all right, but I'm afraid the poor lad is also slightly out of his head."

SHAFTESBURY SEDGWICK'S DINNER AND speech had a sharp effect on Jack Taylor. So did the remarks of Jack's solid geometry teacher, Mr. Foss, a few days later. "Taylor, your mark on that last quiz was the lowest you've hit so far. You're going to flunk solid this month, and at the present rate you're going to flunk your college boards later on. That means that you won't be getting into M.I.T. in the fall. If I were you, I'd give up hockey even though you are the captain and the star of the team. You don't seem to be able to do two things— play hockey and prepare for M.I.T." Mr. Foss smiled rather grimly. "Needless to say, I'd strongly advise you, if faced with a choice, to take the Massachusetts Institute of Technology."

Jack swallowed. "Yes, sir," he said and walked away. He knew that his marks were slipping, and yet Mr. Foss' speech had come as a straight right to the solar plexus. It had knocked Jack's wind out.

Trying to regain his breath, he thought, Give up hockey? Holy smoke, I couldn't do that. I've worked hard to become captain of the Trent team. I've come a long way since those pick-up games on the big pond. Now I'm the star. If I go to St. Barnes and Harvard—that's it. St. Barnes. Suppose I do flunk a couple of college boards this June. Old man Foss thinks I'm doomed if I flunk solid, but I can make it up at St. Barnes. Mr. Sedgwick was right. I was at the crossroads. Well, I'm not now. I'll stick it out as captain of the Trent team. We'll win the championship if I have to do it singlehanded, then St. Barnes and Harvard.

JERRY MASON WAS NOT SURPRISED BY Jack's decision which he heard about indirectly through Mr. Foss. But he was depressed by the news. Now their friendship seemed broken for good. Jerry had hoped that they might forget their differences sooner or later, possibly after the hockey season. But now he realized with regret that there was little chance. He was going one way, Jack was going another. Jerry remembered the numerous times they had talked about M.I.T. and how they had shared an enthusiasm for engineering. But Jerry also

knew that now surface emotions had taken control, and unfortunately they had taken control at a decisive moment. Knowing this, Jerry was downcast when he passed Jack in the school corridors surrounded by his little group of admirers.

Boney Ward, however, was pleased to hear that Jack was not going to M.I.T. At the same time, he was disappointed in Jack's avoidance of any contract commitments. But Boney consoled himself with the thought that Jack might flunk out of St. Barnes or Harvard and come to him begging for a chance to play pro hockey.

But there was one person whose viewpoint was startling. Jack met him on a streetcar in Boston. He saw a profile he recognized, a face that brought back memories of a small boy skating frantically on wobbly ankles to get one more glimpse of a hockey hero. It was Johnny Nolan.

The car was crowded and Jack was pushed near Nolan. He hesitated a moment and then spoke. "Uh, you're John Nolan, aren't you?"

Johnny Nolan looked sideways and down with a quick smile and a nod.

"I used to see you play hockey," said Jack.

"Oh," said Johnny Nolan, still smiling. "That seems like a long time ago."

"I guess it does," said Jack. He had been hoping that Johnny Nolan might recognize him from his picture in the papers, as some people occasionally did, but it was evident that recognition was not forthcoming. Jack said, "I play for Trent. Center. My name's Jack Taylor."

Johnny Nolan put out his hand and smiled. "You do, eh? Glad to know you, Jack. Matter of fact, I think I've

read something about you in the paper. You're captain, aren't you?"

"Yes," said Jack, feeling a warmth rise in him. "I'm in my last year." Then he thought, That's silly. Of course I'm in my last year if I'm captain. But the words just seemed to tumble forth, stimulated by the excitement of this meeting.

"You're going to college, I suppose?" said Nolan.

"Yes," said Jack. "I was going to M.I.T., but just last week I changed my mind and decided to go to prep school for a year. St. Barnes and then to Harvard."

Jack watched Johnny Nolan's face for the expression of approval he expected to see. It did not appear. Instead, curiosity showed itself in Johnny Nolan's face as he turned and said, "Did a man by the name of Shaftesbury Sedgwick have anything to do with this?"

"Why, yes," said Jack. "Yes, he did."

"I see," said Johnny Nolan. "You know, I used to work for Sedgwick. I'd like to talk to you about this. I've got to get off next stop, but if you could come over to Cambridge and see me . . ."

"Sure," said Jack. "I'd be glad to."

"Fine! I'm at 123 Quincy Street. Come on over." Johnny Nolan grinned and started edging his way to the rear door of the car. The car came to a stop. Nolan got off and walked away with some of the ease and grace he had once showed on his skates. Then he disappeared.

Jack thought, I'd better go see him. But that was a queer look in his eye when he said "Shaftesbury Sedgwick." Maybe Mr. Sedgwick was right. Maybe Johnny Nolan is out of his head.

JOHNNY NOLAN DIDN'T SEEM OUT OF HIS head when Jack called on him in Cambridge on a cold and windy day a short while after the encounter on the streetcar. Nolan seemed perfectly normal as he greeted Jack with a strong handshake and a friendly smile. "Come on in, Jack. Make yourself at home. How about some hot tea and a piece of raisin cake?"

"Fine. Thanks."

Jack sat down in a big chair and looked around as Johnny Nolan put a kettle of water on a small electric grill. It was a big room with a fire in the fireplace and a great many books—books all over the place, in bookcases, on tables, on chairs.

"Thought you might be playing. hockey on a day like this."

"Too much wind," said Jack. "Blow you off the ice. Practice tomorrow. By the way, should I call you Mr. Nolan or Captain Nolan? You were a captain, weren't you?"

"Yes, and call me Johnny Nolan," said Nolan, smiling. "Yes, I guess the wind would blow you off the ice today. I forgot about outdoor hockey. I played indoors so many years."

The tea was good and warming and the cake was heavy and full of raisins. So far, thought Jack, he had detected no signs of insanity in the ex-Harvard star.

"As I remember it," said Johnny Nolan, sitting comfortably in a big chair, "you said something about making a decision a short while ago, something about changing your mind."

"That's right." Jack spoke earnestly. "I made up my mind to go to M.I.T. I had a good friend at Trent named Jerry Mason, and he has a cousin who is an M.I.T. grad. We all had dinner together last year down in Chinatown." Thinking back on it, that dinner had been a lot of fun; he hadn't thought about it for a long time; too many other things to think about, mostly connected with ice hockey. "That was really when I decided to go to M.I.T. But this winter my math marks are slipping, and this month I'm sure to flunk solid geometry. So I guess, well, anyway, this St. Barnes-Harvard deal looks pretty good to me," Jack finished lamely.

"And anyway," said Johnny Nolan, "who ever heard of the M.I.T. hockey team?"

"That's right," said Jack and looked up and saw Johnny Nolan smiling at him.

Nolan put his empty teacup on the table. "You had dinner with Shaftesbury Sedgwick at his club and he said he'd send you to St. Barnes?"

"That's right," said Jack. "How'd you know?"

"Because I went to St. Barnes and Harvard under the sponsorship of Mr. Sedgwick. Did he mention me?"

"Yes, uh, he, well, I guess we both did."

Johnny Nolan smiled. "And he said I was out of my head?"

Jack's face reddened. "Well, uh, yes, I guess he did."

Nolan continued to smile. He picked up the cake plate, extended it toward Jack, and put it back on the table. "Did he say something about learning to think at Harvard?"

"Yes, I guess he did."

"I thought so," said Nolan. "The same old double-talk. Listen, Jack. I learned to think, but I didn't learn to think at Harvard. I didn't learn to think at Harvard because I was so full of the-right-club and the-right-people baloney that Sedgwick had been serving up for the last twenty years. I didn't go to Harvard for an education. I went to Harvard to be a hockey star and have a lot of people fall all over my neck after the games at the Garden."

Jack was sitting back in his chair but he was not relaxed. There was nothing about Nolan's voice or words that made him feel the slightest bit sleepy.

"Last year," said Johnny Nolan, "you made up your mind to go to M.I.T. Is that right?"

"Yes, that's right."

"You like engineering? You like the idea of working at that?"

"You bet I do."

"The only reason you want to go to Harvard is to play hockey, to be a star on the Harvard hockey team."

"Well, I guess so," said Jack.

"Then, for heaven's sake," said Nolan sharply, "go home and study geometry."

"But what about Boney Ward? What about Mr. Sedgwick?"

"Listen, Jack!" Nolan spoke rapidly. "Those two birds aren't interested in you. They're interested in themselves. Boney Ward wants to make money out of you—you know that as well as I do. Sedgwick wants to use you as a pawn in the old alumni game which makes him feel like a bigshot standing in the wings moving puppets on a stage. Don't fall for that stuff. I did. And I wasted about five years of my life. Now I've got to start almost all over again. Luckily I've got another chance. And this time I'm going to make the most of it. When I was here in Cambridge as an undergraduate, I used to see things the way Sedgwick saw them, the right people, the right clubs, the right clothes, all that baloney. People like Sedgwick aren't interested in Harvard as an educational institution. They're interested in it as a social club. If you come here under their sponsorship to be a hockey star and a social success, you're not going to get an education. Sedgwick's particular brand of bull was bad enough twenty years ago; today it's dangerous nonsense."

Johnny Nolan got up out of his deep chair and stood in

front of the fireplace with his hands in his pockets. "Does any of this make sense to you?"

Jack stared at him. "You bet it makes sense," he said at last. "I knew Ward was a phony after that run-in I had with him and his pal, the Ripper. I wasn't sure about Sedgwick. St. Barnes and Harvard didn't look like a bad deal the way things were going, but I think I knew all along that I was being a fool to give up M.I.T."

Nolan smiled. "And you were right. I'll guarantee that six years from today when you're working on some engineering project, whether it's in the Missouri Valley or up the Yangtze river, you'll thank your lucky stars that you're not sitting at a desk at Sedgwick, Harrod, and Wigglesby, worrying about whether you're going to land an account and whether or not you're going to be invited to some dinner party." Nolan paused and when he spoke again his voice was lighter and slower, like a hockey player who has just scored and who skates slowly and confidently back up the ice, satisfied with his accomplishment. "Well, now that we've got that straightened out, I want you and your friend, Jerry Mason, to join me in a little hockey next Saturday afternoon. I'll call for you. We'll drive out to a pond I know, out in the country. Bring your hockey sticks and shin pads; I still think I can show you two a couple of tricks about hockey."

THE PHONE RANG IN THE MASON HOME
and Jerry answered.

"Jerry?"

"Yes."

"Jack Taylor."

"Hello, Jack."

"I know how you feel about . . . Listen, Jerry, I just
wanted to say that I'm sorry a lot of things happened.
I've changed my mind . . ."

"What, again?"

"Yes, again. I finally came to. I turned in my uniform
this afternoon.

"You did what?" Jerry's voice had come to life.

"You should have heard Boney. Wow! But it's done,
finished. M.I.T. or bust."

"Well, for gosh sake! I was wondering if you'd ever
come around."

"Well, you can stop wondering."

"O.K., Jack. If you need any help in math, just let me
know."

"Don't worry, I will. See you tomorrow, Jerry."

"You bet."

IT WAS A BEAUTIFUL DAY, CLEAR AND
cold. The green firs and cedars stood up straight against
patches of powdery snow and brown pine needles. The
ice was smooth and black on the pond Johnny Nolan had
picked out. On the way out to the country Jack had described Boney Ward's anger, Mr. Sedgwick's astonish-

ment, and the solid geometry teacher's pleasure at Jack's decision to give up hockey and concentrate on math and M.I.T. Johnny Nolan had smiled and nodded. Jerry had grinned, and Jack had felt a deep feeling of satisfaction in the approval of two sincere friends. Now that the decision had been made, the decisive step taken, a great load seemed to have dropped from his shoulders. The decision had caused a furor in school, but Jack was surprised at how quickly the furor died down—as quickly as the excitement of the hockey season died when spring came.

When they were on the ice of the pond, Johnny Nolan tossed out a puck and said, "O.K., you two play defense. I'll bring it down." Nolan skated away from them with his long, graceful strides and Jack said, "Look at the guy skate." Jerry said, "I'm looking."

Johnny Nolan swerved, cut a half-circle, and came at them flying over the ice, holding his stick lightly in one hand. As he neared them, he put both hands on it and dribbled the puck while he sized up the position Jack and Jerry were taking to stop his rush. Jack crouched, waited, and as the flying figure came within range lashed out with a pokecheck. Magically, the puck and the stick that guided it were just out of reach. Jerry saw a body flash through the air and lunged at it with hip and shoulder. The body left the ice and sailed through the air while the puck slid between the defensemen. Johnny Nolan landed just beyond them on one skate, one hand on his hockey stick, the puck again on the stick. He was through, in the clear—high, wide, and handsome. Jack looked at Jerry and shook his head. "I think I saw someone go by here a minute ago."

Jerry grinned. "Wonder who it was. Think he had a puck with him."

Johnny Nolan slowed down, circled, and came back, skating easily. He skidded to a stop and said to Jack, "O.K., your turn."

Jack hooked the puck on his stick and started to skate up the ice. "Maybe it's just as well I'm not going to Harvard. Maybe I wouldn't have made the team."

Jerry grinned. "Who knows?" he said, and added, "Who cares?"

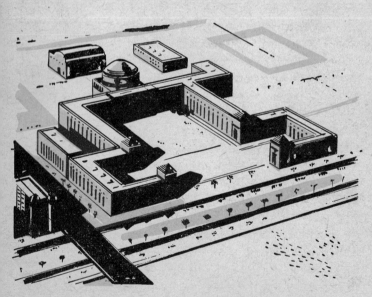

See next page for list of other *Comet* books.

BOOKS

by

Philip Harkins

If you'd like to read other exciting sports and adventure stories by Philip Harkins, you can probably borrow the ones listed below at your school or public library. If you should want to buy them in handsome, cloth-bound editions, visit your local bookstore, or write the original publishers, in New York City.

Published by William Morrow and Company, Inc.

THE BIG SILVER BOWL	$2.50
TOUCHDOWN TWINS	2.50
SOUTHPAW FROM SAN FRANCISCO	2.50

Published by Harcourt, Brace and Company, Inc.

COAST GUARD, AHOY!	$2.00
BOMBER PILOT	2.00

BUILD YOUR OWN COMET BOOK LIBRARY

The Printing History of

LIGHTNING ON ICE

Morrow edition published October, 1946

1st printing .... *August, 1946*
2nd printing .... *June, 1948*

Comet Books edition published October, 1949

1st printing .... *September, 1949*

Designed and produced by the Sandpiper Press

This *Comet* Book includes every word contained in the original, higher-priced edition. It has been printed from new plates made from completely reset, large, clear, easy-to-read type. It is published by arrangement with William Morrow and Company, Inc.

Lightning
on Ice

BY PHILIP HARKINS

Illustrated by
ARTHUR SHILSTONE

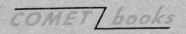

COMET books

ROCKEFELLER CENTER, NEW YORK

2

D0264097